Clarence
Takes a Vacation

Clarence
Takes a Vacation

(Original title: Clarence Turns Sea Dog)

by PATRICIA LAUBER

illustrated by LEONARD SHORTALL

SCHOLASTIC BOOK SERVICES

NEW YORK • TORONTO • LONDON • AUCKLAND • SYDNEY • TOKYO

For Mother,
who hardly got into this book at all,
and for Clarence, who supplied the adventures
and worked very hard at being a companion
while they were being written up

Copyright © 1959 by Patricia Lauber. All rights reserved. Published by Scholastic Book Services, a division of Scholastic Magazines, Inc., by arrangement with the author. First published by Coward-McCann, Inc. in 1959 under the title CLARENCE TURNS SEA DOG. Gateway edition published by Random House, Inc. in 1965.

12 11 10 9 8 7 6 5 4 3 2 1   3   8 9/7 0 1 2 3/8
                                                        11
Printed in the U. S. A.

Contents

A Strange Welcome

THE taxi turned off the highway onto a curving, bumpy road. Immediately, Clarence sensed we were arriving. He whimpered, squirmed, and tried to climb out the window. Brian, my brother, hauled him back and took a firm grip on his collar. "Is this it? Are we there?" Brian asked.

"Almost," the driver said. "You can't see it from here, but the house is set back of those dunes there." He pointed to some sandy hills. "And beyond that's the sea."

Panting with excitement, Clarence tried to climb into the front seat.

"Does your Aunt Josephine know you're bringing your dog?" the driver asked. "Reason I ask is that she didn't say anything about a dog when she asked me to meet you. She just said her car had a flat tire and could I meet the children at the station."

"Of course she knows," Brian said. "Aunt Jo *invited* Clarence. First she invited Mother because she's really Mother's aunt, not ours. Then she said she hoped Sis and Brian (that's me) and Clarence could come, too."

"We thought it was very nice of Aunt Jo," I added. "I mean, not everybody would think to invite Clarence to Cape Cod."

"That's for sure," the driver said. Clarence was licking the back of his neck.

I didn't know quite what he meant. So I said, "Mother couldn't come, but Brian and Clarence and I could."

Brian added, "It's the first time we've ever been on a trip by ourselves. I like traveling alone."

The driver turned by a sign that said McKENZIE, drove on a little farther, then stopped near a big, old-fashioned house.

Clarence scrambled out, tugging impatiently on his leash. The driver took our bags from the trunk, said good-by, and drove away.

"Shall I let Clarence loose?" Brian asked.

I nodded.

Clarence dashed off and vanished among the scrubby trees and bushes.

Brian and I picked up our bags and started for the house. We were nearing the porch steps when the door opened and two women came out. One was short and plump. She had a round, pleasant face surrounded by wisps of gray hair. The other was tall and heavy-set. Her black hair was drawn into a tight bun. There was something about her that made her seem in charge, but I found myself hoping the other one would turn out to be Aunt Jo.

"There," the short one said, "I knew I heard — children, how *are* you?" She kissed both of us. "Goodness, I wouldn't know you — oh, this is my old school friend, Miss Grimes, who's also visiting me. Hortense, here are the children."

"So I see," said Miss Grimes. She looked us up and down. I began to feel that my face was probably dirty and my hair needed combing.

Miss Grimes shook hands. "Are you Brian or Clarence?" she asked Brian.

Brian's jaw dropped.

"He's Brian," I said quickly.

Aunt Jo looked around. "Then where is Clarence? He did come, didn't he?"

"Oh, yes," Brian said. "He's around somewhere."

"We let him go for a run," I explained, "because he's been shut up all day in the baggage car."

"In the *baggage* car?" Miss Grimes said. "What was he doing there?"

We explained that the conductor wouldn't let him travel in the coach with us.

"Mercy!" Aunt Jo said. "What are the railroads coming to?"

"It was all right, really," Brian said. "He didn't mind too much. We visited him and took him drinks of water. And the baggageman let Clarence sit in his lap. After Providence it was very interesting. They had two calves and a pig in the baggage car. Clarence had never met any calves or pigs before and he had quite a good time smelling them and making friends."

"How dreadful!" Miss Grimes said to Aunt Jo. "I don't know why their mother let them travel alone."

"It's a shame your mother couldn't come," Aunt Jo said.

"We almost couldn't come either," Brian said. "Usually we'd be in school in September. But this year school isn't opening until October because of all the mumps in Fairport."

"Urrgh!" Miss Grimes said. She stepped back a little.

"Oh, Brian and I have had mumps," I said.

4

"Has Clarence?" Miss Grimes asked.

Brian and I looked at each other. "No," Brian said, "but I don't think —"

"Where *is* Clarence?" Aunt Jo said. "I hope he hasn't wandered away."

Brian called, "Clarence!" He whistled.

Miss Grimes gave Brian an odd look.

In a moment, Clarence came bounding around the house and ran circles about us. Then he sat down at my feet, tongue hanging out and tail wagging.

"And what is that?" Miss Grimes asked.

"Why, that's Clarence," Brian said.

"But," Aunt Jo said, "in your mother's letters—she just talked about Clarence — she never said —I thought — one of the children."

"Well," Miss Grimes said briskly, "Clarence will just have to be sent away. It is out of the question to have an animal in your lovely house, Josephine. Besides, I am not fond of dogs."

Clarence chose that moment to try to make friends with Aunt Jo. He stood on his hind legs and put his nose in her hand. Aunt Jo stroked his head. "He does have a sweet face," she said to Miss Grimes. "And I don't suppose two children and a dog would be any more trouble than three children and no dog."

"Out of the question," Miss Grimes repeated.

Brian stood up tall. "If Clarence is sent away, I'm going, too."

I wasn't going to let Brian get ahead of me. After all, Clarence is my dog. So I said, "I'll go, too. Love me, love my dog."

"Children, children," Aunt Jo said, hugging us. "Nobody's going to send you away — or Clarence. Of course he can stay."

"Humph!" said Miss Grimes and went into the house.

Aunt Jo said. "You mustn't mind Hortense. She does mean well, you know. Now, bring your things into the house."

"You'll like Clarence," Brian said. "He's very well-behaved."

Aunt Jo opened the door. Clarence, who had been walking quietly at our heels, bounced into the house ahead of us, eager to explore. Ahead of him lay the living room, its shining floor dotted with small oval rugs. Clarence skidded into the living room, jumped on a rug, slid halfway across the floor, jumped off, stopped just short of a table, and skidded into a corner on another little rug. Recovering, he started toward us at top speed, sending two rugs swishing up a wall, while another vanished under a chair.

Brian took a couple of steps forward and grabbed for

Clarence. His feet went out from under him. Brian went down with a thud. A table of ornaments rocked.

"Oh, dear," Aunt Jo said.

Brian clambered to his feet. His face was as red as his hair. "We're sorry, Aunt Jo. At home the floors aren't slippery, but we'll learn to be careful." Brian and I put the rugs back where they belonged.

By this time Clarence had finished exploring and quieted down. He came upstairs and helped us by taking things out of the suitcases and shaking them. At the bottom of Brian's suitcase, Clarence found his toys. At home he had brought us the toys to pack when he saw we were going on a trip. He carried Fish, Ball, and Ring into my room. He arranged them neatly on the old bedspread Mother had sent along for him. Then he lay down and waited for us to get ready for supper.

At the table Miss Grimes talked about people she and Aunt Jo had known at school. Every now and then Brian would try to get into the conversation. He would say something like, "Once Clarence caught a burglar." Aunt Jo would look very interested. But Miss Grimes would just say "Humph!" and start to talk about something else.

After we'd all helped with the dishes, Miss Grimes said, "Television time," and led the way into the study.

Clarence pricked up his ears at the word "television." He is very fond of watching certain programs. He trotted happily after us and when he saw the TV set he wiggled all over with pleasure and jumped into the best chair, right in front of the set.

"That is my chair," Miss Grimes said, sweeping Clarence to the floor and plopping herself down. "Now, Brian, of course you want to see a Western."

"I thought perhaps the children — I mean, I do like —" Aunt Jo began.

"Nonsense, Josephine," Miss Grimes said firmly. "You know we always watch the Westerns."

Aunt Jo turned on the set. "I *do* like music and singing," she said, looking at me.

"That's what I like," I said, "and so does Clarence."

"Don't be silly, Sis," Miss Grimes said. "Dogs don't understand television."

Brian said Clarence loved television. I agreed. Miss Grimes said it was all decided anyhow — we'd voted for a Western.

The sound came on first, and we found ourselves in the middle of a big gun battle. Poor Clarence yipped once, put his tail between his legs, and tried to crawl under the couch. There wasn't room, so he crept into my lap and lay there shivering.

Aunt Jo's face clouded with worry. "Is Clarence ill?"

I explained that Clarence is gun-shy; any loud noise

9

like that frightens him. He hates Westerns.

A sparkle came into Aunt Jo's eyes. "Well," she said, "we can't have Clarence unhappy. After all, he *is* a guest. I invited him here."

"Shall I change the program?" Brian asked.

Aunt Jo nodded.

Brian studied the program guide and found us a good variety show.

Clarence stopped shaking. He sat up and looked at the screen. His tail wagged. He threw back his head and sang along with the performer, "Aourrou, aourrou!"

"Why, he's musical!" Aunt Jo said. "What a loud clear voice!"

Miss Grimes rose. "I think I shall take a little walk before bedtime. Too much television is bad for the eyes." She left the room.

"Humph!" Brian said.

I poked him.

Aunt Jo was happily settling herself in the chair Miss Grimes had left. "Isn't this nice?" she said. "I mean, this is the first time in two months that I've seen anything except a Western. But now that I have more than one guest . . ." She let the sentence trail off.

I was beginning to feel at home. I could see Aunt Jo

was just like Mother about being polite to guests and letting them have their own way. I could also see that as guests, Brian and Clarence and I might be very helpful to Aunt Jo.

Clarence jumped into the chair with Aunt Jo. He settled himself half in the chair and half on her lap.

Aunt Jo stroked him. "I think I'm going to enjoy having a dog here," she said to him. "But do try not to skid the rugs up the walls more than once a day."

2

Clarence Takes Up Collecting

Cᴌᴀʀᴇɴᴄᴇ had never seen waves before, and he didn't know quite what to make of them. He stood close to us and watched. Every minute or so, a wave would roll in toward the beach, break, and run foaming up the sand. Clarence advanced cautiously on some of the white foam. He sniffed at it, discovered it was wet, and quickly drew back. If there is one thing he doesn't like, it's getting wet.

Clarence decided that the beach would be much nicer without waves. So the next time one rolled in, he barked at it. The wave drained off the beach. Clarence gave us a pleased look. He waited for another one, ran barking at it, and chased it out over the wet sand. In no time, he was racing back up the beach, chased by an incoming wave.

"I'm going to make a shell collection," Brian said, running his fingers through the sand.

"So am I," I said. "I'm going to make a shell necklace for Mother and one for Aunt Jo."

"I'm going to see how many different kinds I can collect," Brian said. Then his voice changed. "Oh-oh."

Miss Grimes was coming across the sand. She halted in front of us, flapped her arms a few times, and breathed deeply. "Well, children, I'm glad to see you up and out on this fine morning," she said. "Now, tell me, what are your plans?"

Before we could answer, Miss Grimes said, "Just as I thought — no plans. Well, I have been thinking of things for you to do so that you will make the most of your vacation."

Brian opened his mouth.

"No, don't thank me," Miss Grimes said. "I like helping people, particularly young people."

Brian closed his mouth and swallowed.

"This morning," Miss Grimes went on, "you can start a shell collection."

"But —" Brian began.

"Of course you want to, Brian," Miss Grimes said firmly. "What is a holiday at the seashore without a

13

collection to show to your little friends when you get home?"

"I don't have any little friends," Brian said angrily. "They're all quite big."

Miss Grimes paid no attention. "I shall come back later and see how you are progressing. Now I must get on with my walk."

Brian and I looked at each other. Somehow all the fun had gone out of our idea. We began a halfhearted search for shells.

Clarence gave up chasing the waves and came to see what we were doing. He trotted back and forth with us for a while. He inspected the pile of shells we were making. Then he went off on his own.

When Brian and I came back from a long trip down the beach, we found Clarence lying beside a pile of things. He was panting and hot but looking pleased.

"Hey," Brian said. "Clarence is making a collection, too."

And so he was. Clarence had collected a tangle of seaweed, a piece of cork, the shell of a horseshoe crab, and the sole of an old shoe.

Brian and I were sorting our shells when Miss Grimes came back. Each of us had a small pile of shells that we liked and had decided to keep. Miss Grimes went through them for us and threw out some of them. Then her eye fell on Clarence's collection.

14

"What is that?" she asked.

"That's Clarence's collection," I said.

"Ridiculous!" Miss Grimes said. "Don't bring that mess back to the house."

Actually, we hadn't intended to take Clarence's collection to the house. But now we felt different.

"It's really quite a nice collection, Clarence," Brian said, when Miss Grimes had gone. "It's much more interesting than shells."

Clarence's tail wagged.

"I think," Brian said, "that perhaps you might like to keep the cork and the shell of the horseshoe crab."

Clarence thought so, too. Brian picked them up and carried them home with us. He hid them under some bushes beside the garage. "There," he said, "that's a good place for your collection, Clarence."

Clarence seemed to understand. That very afternoon he came home with an old glove. After he had showed it to us, he trotted away and put it with his other things under the bushes. Then he brought an empty sardine tin, a greasy paper bag, and an old light bulb. Brian and I didn't think so much of these. When Clarence wasn't looking, we put them in the garbage.

Then next morning Clarence branched out. We first learned of this when we met him trotting down the road, carrying a white cap of some sort. A big, red-faced man was hurrying after him. We saw Clarence

15

stop and put the cap down. He backed off a little, tail wagging. The big man advanced slowly and reached for the cap. Clarence grabbed it and ran. Then he let the man catch up with him and they went through the same performance again.

Brian ran forward, caught Clarence, and took the cap from him. It was a white cap with a black visor. Above the visor was a gold anchor.

The man came up. Brian gave the cap one last admiring look and held it out. "Is this yours?" he asked.

I said, "I'm sorry our dog took it and made you chase him."

The man wasn't angry at all. He tried the cap on Brian. It came down over Brian's ears.

"I'm Cap'n Gregory," he said, putting the cap back on his own head. "Who are you? Don't think I've seen you around these parts before."

We introduced ourselves and Clarence, and I explained that we were visiting Aunt Jo. Captain Gregory seemed very interested. "So you're Josie's kin," he said. "That makes me practically your uncle. You'd better call me Uncle Matt just to get in practice. Been thinking of marrying Josie for thirty years," he added.

"Golly," Brian said. "Did you ever ask her?"

"Once or twice," our new uncle said. He pulled a pipe out of his pocket. A small ball of twine and several fishhooks came out with it. "May ask her again one of these years."

He strolled along the road with us, pointing out landmarks. His own house was built on top of a dune and he invited us to come and see him soon. At the edge of Aunt Jo's property he said good-by and shook Clarence's paw. "Thanks for collecting me and introducing your friends," he said to Clarence.

Late that afternoon Brian took me aside. "Come and see what Clarence has collected now," he urged.

I went with him to the garage. During a busy afternoon, Clarence had collected a case for eyeglasses, a handkerchief, and a white wool sock.

At first I was amused. Then I began to feel a tickle of worry in my stomach. These things belonged to somebody. Suppose the owners hadn't wanted Clarence to collect them?

"You know what, Sis? I bet Clarence is going to have the best collection of all," Brian said. "We don't have anything nearly as nice."

"Clarence? Collecting?" Miss Grimes said, looming up suddenly behind us. "I thought I told you—" She broke off as she saw Clarence's collection. "Where did he get those things?"

18

"He found them," Brian said in a small voice.

"Found them indeed!" Miss Grimes said. "He's stolen them. I shouldn't wonder if we have the police at our door before long."

The tickle of worry turned into an awful sick feeling.

"He didn't steal them!" Brian cried. "He wouldn't do such a thing."

"Humph!" said Miss Grimes. "Then how do you explain this?"

There was nothing for it but to start at the beginning and tell her the whole story of Clarence as a collector. At the end I said, "We encouraged him."

"So," Brian said, "it's really our fault, and if the police come we'll take the blame."

"Well," Miss Grimes said to Brian, "perhaps that won't be necessary. *If* you do as I say, I may be able to help you."

Miss Grimes had two ideas. One was that in the morning we should try to follow Clarence and see if he went back to the same place. Then we could return the things and apologize. If that didn't work, we would just have to go from house to house looking for the owners.

When we agreed, she said very well, we'd say no more about the matter. Then she picked the new things out of Clarence's collection and went into the house.

We knew Miss Grimes had told Aunt Jo the whole story. Aunt Jo didn't say anything but just looked sorrowfully at Brian and Clarence and me. That was far worse than anything Miss Grimes could have said. We spent a gloomy evening and went to bed early.

The next morning it was raining, and Clarence hates being rained on. He went out for a few minutes, then hurried back in and lay down by the fire. He made it quite clear that he was not going collecting. Brian and I were willing to go out in the rain, but Aunt Jo wouldn't let us. She said there wasn't *that* much hurry.

The day dragged on. Miss Grimes suggested that Brian and I read some worthwhile books and improve our minds. But we didn't even feel like reading books that weren't worthwhile. Aunt Jo tried to cheer us up. She played games with us and brought out marshmallows for us to toast. Brian toasted some, but only Clarence was interested in eating them. By dinnertime I was almost hoping the police *would* come and take us away.

I guess Brian was thinking the same thing. After dinner we heard a car stop by the house. Brian jumped to his feet and cried, "The police have come!"

He sounded happier than he had all day.

Aunt Jo peered out the window. "No, it's not the police, Brian. It's a man and a woman." She went to the door.

"Miss McKenzie?" a man's voice said. "My name is Tolliver and I'm sorry to disturb you, but I wonder if you have a small brown, white, and black dog with a curly tail here?"

Brian swallowed hard. He gripped Clarence's collar.

"Yes, we do," Aunt Jo said. "But of course it was all a mistake, as I'm sure you'll understand."

"I don't—" the man said, sounding rather confused, "that is —"

Aunt Jo went on, "Please take your things off and come in by the fire."

The Tollivers came in. They were very nice-looking people.

Clarence recognized them at once. He broke away from Brian and ran over to greet them, first leaping into the air around them and then jumping into Mrs. Tolliver's lap when she sat down.

"Is this the dog you mean?" Miss Grimes demanded.

"Yes, it is," Mr. Tolliver said. "That's just the dog we were looking for."

Aunt Jo turned to the Tollivers and said pleasantly, "I think that if we just talk this over you'll see it was all a harmless prank."

The Tollivers looked more and more bewildered.

Mr. Tolliver said, "I think there's some misunderstanding."

"Didn't this dog steal from you?" Miss Grimes asked. She held up the case for eyeglasses. "Isn't this yours?"

"Well, yes, it is," Mrs. Tolliver said. "But he didn't *steal* it. He came up to visit us. After he'd played and made friends, he picked up the case and looked at us as if to ask whether he might take it."

"And," Mr. Tolliver said, "he was so cute that we said, 'Of course, you may take it.' After all, it's easy to buy another case, but it's impossible to buy a look like that."

"You see," Mrs. Tolliver went on, "I'm an artist and I was sketching him — he's a most appealing little dog—"

Miss Grimes made a strangled noise.

The Tollivers went on with their story. Clarence had visited them several times during the afternoon. Mrs. Tolliver had spent the whole time drawing pictures of him and wanted to do some more. She'd hoped Clarence would come back again. When he hadn't, she and her husband had decided to look for him.

"I was hoping," Mrs. Tolliver said, "that you would let him come back tomorrow."

At this point Miss Grimes excused herself and went up to bed.

Then Brian and I told our half of the story.

The Tollivers said they were very flattered that Clarence had wanted to add their possessions to his collection.

Clarence was pleased with all this talk about himself. He brought Fish, his favorite toy, and started a game, giving us turn about at throwing Fish.

Aunt Jo made cocoa and served cookies, and the Tollivers stayed for two or three hours. When they left, they said they hadn't had such a good time since they came to Cape Cod and they certainly hoped to see more of us.

As the Tollivers drove away, Aunt Jo told us that Mrs. Tolliver was a very famous artist. But Aunt Jo also said she thought we'd better stop Clarence from collecting, if we could. Another time he might not be so lucky in his choice of people to collect from.

Brian and I didn't know exactly how to go about this, but as things turned out it wasn't much of a problem.

The next morning Clarence came running home from some place, jumped into his bed, and stayed there. Brian and I were a little worried, but so far as we could tell he wasn't sick or hurt.

The explanation wasn't long in coming. A lobsterman arrived at the back door, holding a basket in one hand. Grinning from ear to ear, he said, "Hear you got quite a collecting dog visiting you, Miss Josephine."

"Gracious, how news spreads!" Aunt Jo said.

"Well," the lobsterman said, "he came to see me just as I was bringing in my catch this morning. First he studied the lobsters. Then he tried to make friends with them — reckon he thought they were sort of wagging their tails when he saw those waving claws. When they wouldn't play, he made his big mistake. He sat down with his back to them and waved that tail of his right under a lobster's nose, so to speak."

"Oh, my," Aunt Jo said.

The lobsterman said, "I don't rightly know whether Clarence collected the lobster or whether the lobster collected him. But it did seem as if he ought to have it, so I brought the lobster along."

Aunt Jo made lobster stew out of it so everyone could have a share, because, as Brian pointed out, Clarence is not a shellfish dog. But after that Clarence gave up collecting anything except friends, which is what he does best anyway.

3

A Very Useful Sort of Dog

Uncle Matt was pacing angrily up and down on the terrace in front of his house. Clarence was pacing with him, trotting at Uncle Matt's heels and looking up at him with a worried expression. This made it rather difficult for Uncle Matt to pace. Every time he reached an end of the terrace and spun on his heels he almost fell over Clarence.

"What has Miss Grimes done now?" Brian asked.

"It would make me too angry to tell you," Uncle Matt said. He paused in front of us. "Woman comes to spend Fourth of July weekend and she's still here in September. What I don't understand is why Josie puts up with her."

I said, "Aunt Jo is like Mother. She thinks you always have to be polite to guests."

25

"Guest!" Uncle Matt exclaimed. "Ha!" He gave up trying to pace and threw himself into a chair. Clarence jumped into his lap.

"The trouble with you," Uncle Matt said to Clarence with mock sternness, "is that you're too friendly. You like everybody. You probably even like *her*."

It was quite true. Clarence was always trying to make friends with Miss Grimes, even though he didn't get very far.

"You could very easily frighten her," Uncle Matt went on. "Like this." He bared his teeth and growled ferociously at Clarence.

It frightened Clarence. He jumped off Uncle Matt's lap and came to sit with us.

"Never mind, Clarence," I said. "We'd rather have you friendly."

Uncle Matt came over and patted Clarence. "Yes," he said. "you're a nice dog even if you won't make yourself useful and get rid of that woman."

The next person who decided that Clarence ought to make himself useful was Miss Grimes. She found us on the beach, where Clarence was chasing a low-flying sea gull.

"I have decided," Miss Grimes announced, "that there is no reason why Clarence should not be made into a useful sort of dog. Though small, he appears intelligent. It would be much better for him to be learning useful activities than chasing birds and waves."

"But Clarence is on his vacation," Brian said.

"He is wasting his time," Miss Grimes said severely. "When I have trained him for you, you will thank me."

Brian tried to speak.

"You needn't worry," Miss Grimes said. "While I have never trained a dog before, I have had years and years of experience training young people. I can promise you that I am firm but fair. Clarence will emerge a better, more useful dog."

The gull had gone out to sea. Clarence, after a couple of barks at a wave, trotted over to join us.

"Come along, Clarence," Miss Grimes said. "I shall first teach you to fetch."

She went off with Clarence at her heels.

"Fetch?" Brian said to me. "Doesn't that mean bringing back something that's been thrown?"

I nodded.

Brian's face cleared. "That's all right then," he said. "Clarence will love being trained. It's going to be just like playing a game of Fish."

Playing Fish is Clarence's favorite game. The rules are very simple. You throw Fish and Clarence brings it back. The game goes on and on and on until you get tired of it and refuse to play.

If anything, Clarence liked being trained even better than playing Fish. Every time he fetched the ball or the stick or the piece of cork Miss Grimes had thrown, he was petted and praised. At the end of the lesson he was praised again and given dog candy.

That is, Miss Grimes thought it was the end of the lesson. Clarence made it plain that he wanted to go on learning. The lesson continued until lunch.

After lunch Miss Grimes went upstairs for her rest. Clarence picked up Fish and padded after her. Pretty soon Brian and I could hear sounds of something being thrown and Clarence scampering after it.

Later in the afternoon Brian and I took Clarence to the beach. We didn't want him to be overtired by all this fetching. But Clarence wouldn't stay with us. He had a short nap, then bounded off to look for his new playmate.

At dinner, Miss Grimes was unusually quiet. She kept her throwing arm in her lap and ate with her left hand.

"I hope you're not overdoing, Hortense," Aunt Jo said kindly.

"In teaching," Miss Grimes said grimly, "one must always take advantage of the pupil's enthusiasm. Also, a dog cannot be expected to realize that the lesson has ended."

Miss Grimes went early to bed. I caught Clarence starting up the stairs with Fish and brought him back.

I thought it would be good for Clarence to watch TV for a change.

In the morning Clarence had Miss Grimes out before Brian and I had even finished breakfast. Miss Grimes, we noted, was throwing left-handed today.

When he saw Brian and me setting off, Clarence thought he might go with us. Miss Grimes thought otherwise. The important thing, she said, was for Clarence to learn to fetch on command, even if he would rather do something else. "Once he learns this," she said, "he will always, always fetch for you."

Brian and I weren't at all sure that we wanted Clarence taught always, always to fetch, because it was hard enough to put an end to a game of Fish without that. But actually it turned out to be quite a good thing.

At noon Aunt Jo, Miss Grimes, and Clarence came down to the beach with a picnic lunch. Aunt Jo sat down on the sand with us. Miss Grimes prepared to sit on a log.

"Watch out!" Brian said to her. "You'll sit on the fish."

Miss Grimes turned to inspect the log. On it was a dead fish, warming in the sun.

"Is that your fish?" Miss Grimes asked Brian.

"Not exactly," Brian explained. "That is, I didn't catch it. I found it on the beach. I'm leaving it in the

29

sun because I thought it would be interesting to see—"

"Ugh!" said Miss Grimes. She picked the fish up by its tail. "Disgusting!" She tossed it away.

In a flash, Clarence was after it. He brought the fish back and proudly laid it at Miss Grimes's feet.

The fish was pretty smelly. I said, "No, Clarence!"

Miss Grimes held up her hand. "Please do not interfere, Sis, or you will undo all my good work. After all, Clarence has been taught to fetch."

Aunt Jo got a whiff of the fish and wrinkled her nose. "Perhaps this should be an exception," she suggested.

"Clarence does not understand exceptions," Miss Grimes said. "I shall get rid of the fish without throwing it." She walked down to the water's edge and put the fish in the sea. "There," she said, "the tide will carry it out." She rinsed her fingers and started back up the beach.

Clarence hesitated. He put one paw in the water and hastily took it out. He looked reproachfully at Miss Grimes's back. Then he waded into the water, grasped the fish, and ran up the beach. By the time Miss Grimes reached us, Clarence was waiting for her with the fish.

"I thought you said he doesn't like water," Miss Grimes said to us.

"He doesn't," Brian said. "He hates getting wet. He would never have gone in the water except that you trained him so well."

A sickly smile spread across Miss Grimes's face. "Good dog, Clarence," she said.

Clarence wiggled all over.

"Really, Hortense," Aunt Jo protested, "I think this is going too far. Surely Clarence can be told—"

"A dog has limited intelligence—"

"Clarence doesn't either! He's very intelligent!" Brian cried.

"He understands only what I have taught him," Miss Grimes said. "I am trying to turn him into a useful dog and I do not want him confused. I shall dispose of the fish later when he isn't looking."

Aunt Jo, Brian, and I had our lunch to one side. Miss Grimes had hers with Clarence and the fish. Afterward, Brian, Aunt Jo, and I took Clarence back to the house. Miss Grimes stayed behind with the fish.

"I don't think Mother is going to like it if Miss Grimes teaches Clarence to fetch dead fish," Brian said.

"She means well," Aunt Jo said. "And you can see she's terribly fair."

Miss Grimes came back from the beach and washed her hands. "There," she said. "I've buried it." She went upstairs to take her rest.

Clarence sniffed around a little. Then he tracked Miss Grimes's footsteps back to the beach.

When Miss Grimes got up, Clarence was waiting for her with the fish. She pretended not to notice and strolled off into the garden. Clarence picked up the fish and followed her.

A bit later we caught a glimpse of Miss Grimes tiptoeing round the corner of the house. And not long after that we found Clarence sitting beside a big outdoor garbage can. He scratched at the can and looked hopefully at us.

Brian lifted the lid and looked in. First he said, "Ooff!" Then he said with a grin, "Now Clarence has found it, I'll have to hand the fish to him. Otherwise I'd be undoing Miss Grimes's good work."

Clarence snatched the fish and carried it off to Miss Grimes.

While the rest of us were watching television, Miss Grimes was outside building a small fire. There was an odor of cooking fish in the air. Then Miss Grimes went to bed.

When she came down in the morning, Clarence was waiting for her outside the house. He laid a fish at her feet, then backed off expectantly, waiting for her to throw it.

"Where did that fish come from?" Miss Grimes demanded.

"From the beach," Brian said. "When Clarence couldn't find the other fish he went down to the beach and got this one. There are lots of fish on the beach this morning," he added.

Miss Grimes turned pale. "Good dog," she said weakly and went into the house.

Brian and I held a council of war. Partly we were wondering how long Miss Grimes could hold out. But we were also wondering how long *we* could hold out. Clarence himself was beginning to smell rather strongly of fish.

Matters came to a head when Clarence got into the house with the milkman. Aunt Jo, who had been dusting upstairs, came down. Her lips were pressed into a thin line and she went straight after Miss Grimes, who was sitting in the study with the door closed.

"Hortense," Aunt Jo said, "you have gone too far."

Miss Grimes looked startled.

"I never criticize a guest," Aunt Jo said, "but this is too much."

"What have I done?" Miss Grimes said.

"I suppose," Aunt Jo said, "that if you wish to play with a dead fish out of doors, that is your concern. But, Hortense, I will not permit you to keep the fish in your bedroom."

Miss Grimes gaped at Aunt Jo.

"Don't argue with me," Aunt Jo said. "I simply will not permit it. Now kindly take that fish outdoors."

"But I'm not — I didn't —" Miss Grimes said.

Aunt Jo just looked at her.

Miss Grimes left the room.

"Humph!" Brian said.

Aunt Jo sank into a chair. "Gracious," she said in a whisper, "I've never talked to Hortense that way before. I never dared. Even when we were girls in school —perhaps I should—no," Aunt Jo said firmly, "I will not."

Brian and I looked at each other.

Aunt Jo caught the look. "Oh, I know Clarence put it there, but he was only doing what she taught him."

Miss Grimes left that very afternoon, saying that her sister in Boston had been urging her to come for a visit. Clarence was terribly sorry to see her go. He had just found her a particularly fine fish on the beach.

Fortunately, Clarence is a very intelligent dog. So Brian and I were able to un-teach him about fetching fairly quickly. We simply said, "No!" several times in a firm, loud voice.

Aunt Jo gave him a portion of steak for un-learning so well. Then she petted him and said he was really a very useful sort of dog.

4

Buried Treasure

CLARENCE was tracking. Nose to the sand, he was stalking a small sand crab. When the crab stopped, Clarence stopped and pointed. When the crab scuttled forward, Clarence followed. He was concentrating so hard that he didn't even notice when someone came over the dune and sat down beside Brian and me.

The new arrival was a boy we'd seen around. He was about our age, but he was much bigger than Brian. The boy said, "I'm Speed Armstrong. Who are you?"

When we'd told him, he looked at Clarence. "Is that your dog?"

"Yes," I said, "that's Clarence."

Speed hooted with laughter. "Clarence! What a name for a dog! Who ever heard of a dog called Clarence?"

"It's a very good name for a dog," Brian said angrily. "I bet you don't even have a dog."

"I've got something better," Speed said. "I'm building a rocket. As a matter of fact, you're sitting on my rocket site."

Brian and I looked around.

"I mean," Speed said, "when I finish building my rocket, I'm going to launch it from here."

"That's dangerous," Brian said. "You might blow yourself up."

"Of course it's dangerous," Speed boasted. "But I'm not afraid. I bet you're a sissy—and so's your dog. Any dog with a name like Clarence is bound to be."

Brian scrambled to his feet. "I'll show y —"

Speed paid no attention to Brian. "You should see Boy. He belongs to our next-door neighbor, and he's a *real* dog. He's huge and he has great big bulging muscles that ripple when he walks."

"I imagine he's stupid," Brian said. "All muscle and no brain." As he spoke, he looked meaningfully at Speed's muscles.

"No, he isn't," Speed said. "He's very highly trained. All you have to do is say the word and he attacks."

"What word?" I asked.

Speed didn't answer.

"Yah!" Brian said. "You don't even know."

"Of course not," Speed answered. "Boy was right there while Mr. Gunn was telling me. If he'd said the word, Boy might have torn my arm off. Gosh, he's almost bitten the mailman, the milkman, and the boy from the grocery store. None of them will even deliver any more," Speed said admiringly. "Sometimes Mr. Gunn lets me take Boy out. I and he are the only two people who can handle Boy."

"Pooh!" I said. "Who wants a dog like that?"

"*I* do," Speed said. "When the Government buys my rocket plans from me, I'm going to buy a big dog just like Boy."

Brian and I looked at each other. Then Brian said, "I don't believe you have a rocket. I think you're making it up."

Speed laughed. "Well, I'm not going to prove it by showing you my rocket. All important rocket work is top secret. Nobody's seen my rocket and nobody even knows where I work on it, except Boy. Sometimes I take him along to stand guard." Speed looked back at Clarence. "What's he doing now?"

"He's tracking," I said.

"Clarence has quite a few kinds of very valuable dog in him," Brian said. "That's why he's such a good hunter and tracker. See how he points?"

"Points?" Speed said. "Dogs don't point with their hind paws. They point with their front paws."

"Most dogs do," Brian said, "because they only know how to point with their front paws. Clarence can point with any paw."

Just then the crab went down its burrow. Clarence began to dig furiously. Pretty soon all we could see of him was his hind quarters.

Brian said, "Clarence is a very good digger."

I said, "Clarence is good at everything."

Not to be outdone, Brian said, "In fact, Clarence is so good at hunting and tracking and digging that I'm going to use him to hunt buried treasure."

Speed howled with laughter and fell over backward. "Ah-ha-ha! That's the funniest thing I've ever heard — using a dog to hunt buried treasure."

"I don't see what's so funny about it," Brian said. "It's a good idea."

"That's all you know!" Speed snorted. "It's so silly that I'd bet my rocket Clarence couldn't find any buried treasure if he stayed here for a hundred years."

"All right!" Brian said. "We'll show you."

Just then Clarence gave up digging for the sand crab and trotted toward us.

For a moment, I almost wished Clarence was the kind of dog who bit strangers. But he loves meeting people, so he jumped all over Speed and licked his face.

Speed held Clarence off and studied him. "He's pretty small," Speed said thoughtfully.

"But very intelligent," I said.

"His tail curls just right," Speed went on.

"Right for what?" Brian asked.

"Right for fitting into my rocket. You've got to have a small dog with a curly tail — the way the Russians did."

I gasped.

Even Brian was speechless.

Speed got up. "Be seeing you," he said and strolled off.

Brian found his voice. "Not if we see you first," he said, but Speed was gone.

That evening we went to see Uncle Matt and told him the whole story. Uncle Matt didn't think we had much to worry about. "Speed's a regular teller of tall tales," Uncle Matt explained. "Just last year he told everybody he was raising a tiger. Turned out to be a plain, ordinary cat that was tiger striped. Like as not," Uncle Matt said, "Boy is a Pekingese and the rocket's a burned-out firecracker."

We felt much better after hearing that. So Brian brought up the matter of hunting buried treasure. He told Uncle Matt about the bet. "I was just boasting back when I said it," Brian confessed. "But it does seem like a pretty good idea."

Uncle Matt didn't know of any buried treasure around these parts. But he suggested we talk to Mr. Tolliver. "He's interested in the history of the Cape," Uncle Matt explained. "Maybe he's turned up something in all those old books and maps he has."

The next morning we went to see the Tollivers. Mr. Tolliver agreed with Uncle Matt that our chances of finding buried treasure were pretty slim. And he laughed at the idea of Speed sending Clarence up in a rocket. "Why," he said, "it would take the U.S. Army and half a dozen top scientists to do that."

Mrs. Tolliver, though, was indignant. "The very idea," she said. "Imagine even joking about sending Clarence up in a rocket!" Then she went away and brought out a big bone with huge chunks of meat on it. "I was going to make soup from this," she said, "but I can always get another one. May Clarence have it?"

It was the most beautiful bone Clarence had ever had. He took it into the shade and began to work on it. He was still chewing by the time Brian and I were ready to leave. The Tollivers said Clarence was welcome to stay and finish his bone. But Clarence decided he'd rather come with us and bring his bone.

It wasn't easy going, for the bone was big and Clarence's mouth is small. Clarence kept having to lay the bone down and take a fresh grip on it. Brian and I both offered to carry the bone. But Clarence thought so highly of it that he wouldn't trust it even to us.

We were heading home along the beach when someone hailed us. There was Speed coming down the dunes. Beside him, on the end of a chain, stalked a huge dog.

Brian and I stood and stared. Clarence, who was standing near us, laid down his bone on the sand. Then he went forward, tail wagging, to sniff at Boy.

Boy snarled.

Speed tightened his grip on the chain. "You better keep your dog away," he warned.

Brian scooped up Clarence.

"Isn't Boy something?" Speed asked. "Did you ever see such a dog?"

At that moment, Boy lunged. Speed managed to hang onto the chain, but it didn't matter. Boy had seized Clarence's bone.

Clarence squirmed and whimpered in Brian's arms. "You give that back!" Brian said. "That's Clarence's bone."

"Tough!" Speed said.

"That's stealing," I said. "Mrs. Tolliver gave that bone to Clarence."

"I can't give it back," Speed said. "You don't think Boy's going to give it up, do you?"

"I thought you could handle Boy," Brian said.

"I can!" Speed insisted. "But there's no need to. My rocket's almost ready now. And there isn't room for Clarence *and* the bone." Speed strolled off with Boy and the bone.

We had to carry Clarence home to keep him from going after Boy. Clarence was very unhappy. We were unhappy, too. Speed hadn't been exaggerating. Boy was just as big and fierce as he had said. And this meant that he might be building an honest-to-goodness rocket.

When Aunt Jo heard what had happened, she gave Clarence a plate of chicken meat at lunch and promised him a new bone. Clarence soon cheered up.

Brian and I were still worried, though. And you can imagine what we felt like when Clarence disappeared. One minute he was poking around in some bushes. The next minute he was gone. We called and whistled, but he didn't come. We telephoned all the friends he might be visiting. But Clarence had vanished.

Brian was all for calling the police and having Speed arrested. I thought we'd better ask Uncle Matt first.

Uncle Matt listened to our story. Then he said, "Well, even if Speed wasn't exaggerating about Boy, that still doesn't prove he's planning to send Clarence up in a rocket."

"Then where is Clarence?" I asked. "He never goes

wandering off for the whole afternoon this way."

"Please can't we call the police?" Brian begged.

Uncle Matt thought. "Tell you what," he said. "Suppose we start by calling Speed's family." He went to the phone. "Mrs. Armstrong?" we heard him say. "This is Matthew Gregory. Is Speed home? No, I wanted to ask him . . . What?" A look of concern came over Uncle Matt's face. "He did? No, Brian and Sis saw them this morning. Just a minute."

Uncle Matt turned to us. "Speed has disappeared," he said. "Boy came home alone before noon. But nobody's seen Speed since this morning. Where was he when you saw him?"

We described the place as best we could.

Uncle Matt repeated what we'd said. "All right, we'll meet him there." He hung up the phone. "Come on," he said to us. "Mrs. Armstrong called the police. We're going to meet Sergeant Wood on the beach where you saw Speed this morning."

The sergeant was waiting for us beside a jeep that he had driven along the wet sand. We told him the whole story.

The sergeant frowned thoughtfully and stared down the beach. "Did you think they were going to the secret rocket place this morning?"

"I thought so," I said, "but Speed didn't really say."

Uncle Matt had a suggestion. "What about getting this dog Boy to lead you to the place?"

"I tried that," the sergeant said, "but he just snarled at me and went back to sleep. He didn't seem to get the idea at all."

"Clarence could track Speed," Brian said. "If we could find Clarence, he could find Speed. Can't we look for Clarence first?"

The sergeant grinned and ruffled Brian's hair. "We'll look for them both at the same time. Hop into the jeep and we'll take a drive along the beach."

As Uncle Matt, Brian, and I watched for signs of Speed and Clarence, the sergeant told us that Speed's family didn't know anything about his rocket. What had started them worrying was Speed's absence at lunch. Speed might vanish for hours at a time, but he never missed a meal.

Sergeant Wood had hardly finished telling us all this, when Brian shouted, "Look, Sis! There's Clarence! I see him!"

Far down the beach a small dog was standing on the sand looking in our direction. The sergeant stepped on the gas. When he stopped, Brian and I piled out of the jeep. It was Clarence! He was perfectly fine except that he seemed a little tired. He also had something on his mind. As soon as he'd greeted all of us, he trotted

off a few steps and then looked back at Brian and me to see if we were coming.

We followed him up the beach. The dunes here were very high. At their foot was a great pile of sand with some planks and beams sticking out of it. Clarence had spent the afternoon digging here. There were holes in the pile of sand, holes in the beach around it.

Uncle Matt and Sergeant Wood looked at all this. Then they looked at each other.

The sergeant said, "Wasn't there a hut here once?"

Uncle Matt nodded. "Belonged to some fisherman. Then in that bad storm two or three winters ago, the dunes shifted. The hut was swallowed up in sand."

The sergeant said thoughtfully, "Do you suppose—"

"Might be," Uncle Matt said. "I don't think the whole hut collapsed."

Looking very concerned, the sergeant hurried toward the remains of the hut. "Ahoy!" he yelled.

A faint voice called, "Help!"

"Speed!" the sergeant yelled. "You in there?"

"Yes," the muffled voice replied.

Sergeant Wood ran back to the jeep for shovels. Then, working with great care, he and Uncle Matt began to dig.

Clarence was delighted. He began to dig, too.

In a matter of minutes, Sergeant Wood, Uncle Matt, and Clarence had made a big hole. Speed crawled out through it. Clarence went on digging as Sergeant Wood pulled Speed to his feet.

"You all right?" he demanded.

"I guess so." Speed was blinking and squinting in the light.

"Of all the fool things to do!" Uncle Matt said. "What did you do — blow the place up with your rocket?"

"No," Speed said in a small voice. "I couldn't. I mean, it wasn't a real rocket. It was just a model."

"Then what happened?" the sergeant demanded.

Speed explained that a few months ago he had discovered the hut buried in sand and tunneled into it. Part of the hut had collapsed but part was still standing. Speed had shored up the opening and used the hut as a secret place to keep his rocket. Everything had been fine until this morning.

"Boy found a bone," Speed said.

"He did not," Brian said. "He stole it from Clarence."

Speed blinked in Brian's direction. "Oh," he said, "are you here? I still can't see in the light."

"All right," the sergeant prompted. "Boy had a bone."

"Well," Speed went on, "I didn't see what hap-

49

pened, but I guess he decided to bury it. I heard him digging near me. The next thing I knew the tunnel was collapsing and Boy was gone."

"Weren't you scared?" Brian asked.

"A little," Speed admitted. "But I knew Boy would save me. First he went away. When he couldn't get help he came back. He's been trying to dig me out for two or three hours."

"Boy!" Sergeant Wood snorted. "It's Clarence who's been trying to dig you out. Boy buried you along with his bone and then went home and forgot about both of you. If it hadn't been for Clarence you might have been here for a week before we found you." He took Speed by the arm. "Come on. Your mother's sick with worry."

Uncle Matt drove off with them. Brian and I said we'd walk home with Clarence. This time Clarence let me carry the bone, which he'd found shortly after Uncle Matt and Sergeant Wood had rescued Speed.

The next day Mrs. Armstrong came to call on us, bringing Speed. She wanted to meet Clarence and Brian and me and to thank us for rescuing Speed. Then she made Speed apologize for having said he was going to send Clarence up in a rocket.

Red-faced, Speed said he was sorry. "I was only teasing," he explained, squatting and patting Clarence. "I like dogs. I wouldn't really do a thing like that." Clarence took a nip at Speed's nose. "Golly," Speed said, "Clarence likes me and I like him. We're friends. I wouldn't hurt him."

Mrs. Armstrong had brought Clarence a new collar. Attached to it was a little medal that read: CLARENCE — *for bravery.* She sent Speed to the car for a huge box, which he gave to Brian. It was a model rocket kit.

Brian didn't know what to say.

Mrs. Armstrong said, "Speed told me about your bet."

"But —" Brian began.

"Oh, I know," Mrs. Armstrong said. "You think of buried treasure as a chest of jewels. But Speed is my treasure."

Speed's face turned fiery red. "Aw, Ma," he said. "Cut it out."

For the first time I began to feel sorry for Speed. I mean, our mother may think Brian and I are treasures, but she'd never say so in public like that.

After the Armstrongs had left, Brian took me aside for a talk. Finally we decided to put the problem to Aunt Jo and Uncle Matt.

"I don't think I should keep the rocket kit," Brian said.

"And Clarence isn't sure he should keep the medal," I said.

"Gracious," Aunt Jo said, "why not?"

"Because Clarence had tracked Boy and was just trying to find his bone," I explained.

"And neither the bone nor Speed is really treasure," Brian added.

Aunt Jo and Uncle Matt said nothing.

"Mother likes us to be honest," I said.

Aunt Jo smiled at us. "I think you could keep them," she said. "You must remember that treasure can mean different things to different people. Mrs. Armstrong would much rather have Speed than a chest of jewels. And Clarence would rather have his bone."

"Besides," Uncle Matt said, "you don't know that Clarence was just digging for his bone. He may have known that Speed was trapped. After all, he's a very intelligent dog."

That was certainly true. In fact, the more we thought about it, the more we began to believe that Clarence had been trying to rescue Speed. Anyway, that was the story printed in the town newspaper the following week. It had a big headline on the front page:

DOG SAVES LOCAL BOY

Then there was a long story about how Speed had been buried. It told how Clarence had tried to dig

Speed out. Sergeant Wood told how Clarence had led the search party to the buried hut. Then Speed was quoted as saying what a fine, brave, intelligent dog Clarence was. At the very end, Speed said. "I'm going to get me a dog just like Clarence."

"Humph!" Brian said when he read that. "There aren't any dogs just like Clarence."

5

Animal Trainer

Brian and Clarence had been racing each other down the road. When I caught up with them, I found them staring over a picket fence into somebody's garden. That is, Brian was staring over it; Clarence was looking through the pickets.

"Sis," Brian said, "there's a talking bird in here. Come listen."

Just as I joined them a man appeared on the other side of the gate. "Hullo," he said, surprised to see all of us.

Behind him a voice said, "Good Polly! Clever Polly! Ah-ha-ha!"

"We were just listening to your bird talk," Brian explained. "I hope you don't mind."

"Not a bit," the man said. "Come in and see Polly, if you like." He swung open the gate and caught sight of Clarence. "Why, you must be Brian and Sis and Clarence."

Now we were surprised. But it turned out that this was Mr. Webster, a very old friend of Uncle Matt's. And that was how he'd heard about us.

We followed Mr. Webster into the garden. On a table in the shade was a cage containing a large green parrot. When she saw us she called, "Beautiful day! Good Polly! Polly, Polly, Polly!"

Clarence was simply fascinated. He climbed onto a chair beside the table and took a seat. Ears pricked up and head cocked, he waited to hear what this astounding bird was going to say next.

Polly hopped onto her swing and preened her feathers, glancing at Clarence from time to time to see if he was watching. Then she said, "Nice pussy! Here, pussy, pussy, pussy!"

Clarence was very impressed. Polly did it again, "Here, pussy, pussy, pussy! Nice pussy!"

"Now watch," Mr. Webster said to us. "Unless you see it, you'd never believe a bird could be so silly."

In a moment we saw what he meant. A big gray cat

came stalking out of the bushes. Its eyes flicked about. Its tail twitched. Like a gray streak the cat sprang to the table. One of its paws shot through the bars of the cage.

"Awk! Help! Awk! Awk!" Polly cried.

Mr. Webster was on his feet, but Clarence moved faster. With a growl, he jumped from the chair to the table. Then everything happened so fast that all I could see was a blur of colors — gray, white, black, brown, and green.

When things settled down, Mr. Webster was holding Polly's cage, and Clarence had treed the cat.

"That was a close one," Mr. Webster said. "Who'd have thought that cat would go after Polly with all of us right here?"

Polly pretended nothing had happened. She preened her feathers and then said, "Good Polly! Clever Polly!"

"You talk too much and you are neither good nor clever," Mr. Webster said severely. "It will serve you right if the cat eats you one fine day."

"Did you teach her to talk?" I asked.

"Yes, I taught her everything except that nonsense about calling the cat," Mr. Webster said. "She picked that up by listening to the woman next door."

"I wish we had a talking parrot," Brian said. He paused. "Or what would be better yet, I wish

Clarence could talk." He turned to Mr. Webster. "Can dogs learn to talk?"

"I don't really know," Mr. Webster said. "But surely you don't want a talking dog. If I were you, I'd leave well enough alone."

"Besides," I pointed out, "Clarence can almost talk. We always know what he's thinking and what he wants. Look at him now."

Clarence had discovered a box of cookies on the ground near the table. He looked at the box. Then he looked at Mr. Webster and back again at the cookie box. He licked his whiskers and sniffed in the direction of the cookies. He looked again at Mr. Webster.

"Obviously he wants a cookie," Mr. Webster said. Clarence's tail wagged at the word. Mr. Webster passed the cookies to us and then gave one to Clarence. "You're a good dog, Clarence," he said. "You deserve a reward for chasing that cat."

"Could Clarence's reward be learning to talk?" Brian asked. "Please?"

"I don't know—" Mr. Webster began.

"I mean, could you try to teach him?" Brian went on. "You taught Polly, and Clarence is very intelligent. Would you try?"

Mr. Webster chewed his lower lip and studied Clarence. I supp—"

At that moment it happened.

Clarence looked from the cookie box to Mr. Webster and said quite plainly, "Cookies."

Brian and I gasped.

Mr. Webster shook his head, "Cookies, *please*."

He and Clarence gazed into each other's eyes. Clarence licked his lips, hesitated, and finally got it out: "Cookies, please."

"That's a good dog," Mr. Webster said.

Brian and I were speechless.

Mr. Webster opened the box and fed Clarence two cookies. Then he put the box in the house, saying, "That's enough for one day."

"I don't," Brian said, "I don't —" He was so astonished that he couldn't get the words out.

Mr. Webster understood. "An animal, like a child, may be ready to talk, but doesn't until something special happens and starts him. Probably it was meeting Polly that started Clarence. He listened to her and thought if she could talk so could he."

"Will Clarence go on talking?" I asked.

"I should think so, though he'll need expert help."

"Could you — would you help him?" Brian asked. "It would be wonderful if Clarence could talk. Please help him."

"Well," Mr. Webster said, "I'm a very busy man — I'm writing a book. But I guess I could spare the time to help Clarence, if that's what you really want."

"More than anything," Brian said.

"Clever girl, Polly!" Polly squawked. Then she said, "Foaming action, foaming action, foaming action! Ha-ha-ha!"

"That reminds me," Mr. Webster said, walking us toward his gate. "Talking animals should be kept away from radios and TV sets so they don't start learning the commercials."

We thought it was probably too late in Clarence's case. But Brian was bubbling over with ideas about putting Clarence *on* television and earning thousands and thousands of dollars and all the things we were going to buy with the money. But he agreed when I suggested that we keep Clarence's talking a secret until Clarence was ready to perform in public. Otherwise, of course, people would just laugh when we said we had a talking dog. And Clarence hates being laughed at.

For the first few days everything went well. We took Clarence to Mr. Webster's each morning for a lesson. And once he'd started talking, Clarence made rapid progress. For example, Mr. Webster and Clarence would sit looking at each other, and the conversation would go something like this:

Mr. Webster: Well, Clarence, how are you today?

Clarence: Hungry.

Mr. Webster: Hungry? Why, you're always hungry. Don't they feed you at home?

Clarence: They forget.

Mr. Webster: You poor little dog! You're probably starving.

Brian: Clarence, that's not so. We never forget to feed you.

Clarence (*looking reproachfully at Brian*): Poor starving little dog.

Brian (*indignantly*): You're not! You're the one who's forgotten.

Clarence: Can't forget hunger.

Mr. Webster: Well, we can't have that. Would you like a cookie?

Clarence (*jumping to his feet*): Would I!

And there the lesson would end. Mr. Webster would pass the cookies. Then Clarence would wander off to visit Polly while we chatted.

Brian was a little disturbed about some of the things Clarence said. On the third day, as soon as Clarence was out of earshot, Brian complained, "We don't forget to feed him! Why does he keep saying that?"

"Well," Mr. Webster said, "it's probably hard for him to remember when he had his last meal."

Brian was still brooding. "What will people think if he goes around saying that?"

Mr. Webster shrugged. "That's the trouble with

talking animals. There's no telling what they'll say."

A slight cloud passed over Brian's face. I knew what he was thinking. Suppose Clarence told millions of people in the TV audience that he was a poor starving little dog. I could just imagine the kind of letters we'd receive from people accusing us of taking the poor little dog's earnings and then not giving him enough to eat.

Meanwhile, Mr. Webster had a problem of his own. Clarence and Polly were becoming very good friends and they'd worked up a game that they played. Polly called, "Here, pussy, pussy, pussy! Nice pussy!" And when the cat came, Clarence chased it and barked while Polly laughed. Mr. Webster wasn't very happy about the game. "Polly's going to be sorry," he said.

As a matter of fact, we weren't completely happy either. You might think it would be wonderful to have a talking dog, but somehow it changes things.

First, temptation became too strong for Brian. We had promised Mr. Webster that we wouldn't try to make Clarence talk at home. Mr. Webster said it would confuse him to have more than one teacher. Also, he didn't want Clarence to overdo talking and strain his throat.

This seemed very sensible. So I was angry when I came upon Brian behind the garage, trying to make

Clarence talk. Brian was sitting on the ground, staring into Clarence's eyes the way Mr. Webster did. "What's your name?" he was saying over and over again to Clarence. When Clarence didn't answer, Brian said helpfully, "Is it Albert? Is it George? Is it Clarence?" At the last question, Clarence wagged his tail.

Tiptoeing away, I decided to teach Brian a lesson. When I saw him a little later, I said, "What do you mean trying to make Clarence talk when you promised not to?"

Brian flushed. "How did you find out?"

I looked Brian straight in the eye. "Clarence told me."

Brian's jaw dropped. Then he recovered and said, "You broke the promise, too."

"No, I didn't. I didn't ask him to speak. He just came and told me."

Brian glared at poor Clarence. "Tattletale!" he said and stamped off.

At first I was very pleased. I started to share the joke with Clarence, but then I thought better of it. I didn't want him blurting out the truth in front of Brian and Mr. Webster. My pleasure changed to unhappiness. Brian and I have always shared secrets with Clarence and talked to him when we needed to get something off our chests. But if Clarence was going to talk, we'd have to stop.

Clarence sensed my feelings and thought he had done something wrong. He crept off and spent the rest of the afternoon with Aunt Jo.

Aunt Jo also knew there was something wrong. She came to find us before dinner and said, "Now, children, make up. You won't enjoy your meal in a bad temper."

"We're not really in a bad temper," I said. "We just —"

"Yes, you are," Aunt Jo said, smiling. "I know. A little bird told me."

Brian and I both looked at Clarence.

Clarence shrank back against Aunt Jo, puzzled and hurt.

Just then Uncle Matt arrived. "Heard there was roast beef for dinner," he boomed. "So I thought I'd stop by and see if any invitations were being handed out."

"Gracious," Aunt Jo said, "how did you find that out?"

"Word gets around, eh, Clarence?" Uncle Matt winked at him.

That was too much for Brian. "It's not fair!" he burst out. "Clarence talks to everybody except me. I hate this. I wish we'd never started it."

"Here, here," Uncle Matt said. "What's all this?"

We told him, and somehow just the telling made me feel better. At the end, Brian said, "You see, it *isn't* fair. Why should Clarence talk to Sis and you and Aunt Jo but not to me?"

I confessed. "Clarence didn't talk to me. I made it up to teach you a lesson."

Aunt Jo said, "And he didn't talk to me. Goodness, nobody had to tell me there was something wrong. It was written all over your faces."

We all looked at Uncle Matt. He grinned and said, "I could smell the roast beef practically up at my place. An old bachelor is likely to be pretty good at sniffing out a tasty dinner."

Brian put his arms around Clarence. "I'm sorry for all the mean things I was thinking," he said.

Clarence was very happy to be out of disgrace. He nibbled Brian's ears and bit him gently on the nose.

"I wish," I said, "that there was some way we could teach Clarence not to talk any more."

"So do I," Brian said. "He was just right almost talking but not quite saying anything."

Uncle Matt nodded. "I agree. Tell you what. Why don't you go along and see Charlie Webster after dinner? Tell him how you feel and ask him to help you."

I didn't know how anybody could stop Clarence

from talking. But the twinkle in Uncle Matt's eyes seemed to promise that Mr. Webster could.

Mr. Webster was reading in his living room when we arrived. Polly's cage hung by the window with a cover over it. I had a strange feeling that he knew what we wanted even before we spoke.

I said, "Mr. Webster, is there any way to stop an animal from talking?"

Mr. Webster said, "You mean you don't want a talking dog?"

"No," Brian said, "we'd rather have Clarence the way he was. We'd rather he just talked with his eyes and tail. We want to be able to tell him secrets and not have to worry about what he may say later."

"We're sorry," I went on, "after all the trouble you've gone to."

Mr. Webster smiled. "Perhaps I can help." After a moment's thought, he turned to Clarence. "What do you think of people who believe in talking dogs?"

"Pretty silly," Clarence said, scratching his ear.

Brian stared at Clarence. "But —"

"And what's the best way to stop a dog from talking?"

Clarence picked out a comfortable chair and jumped into it. "Stop believing." He yawned and lay down.

"Oh!" I said, suddenly understanding.

"*You're* doing it," Brian said. "Clarence isn't talking at all. You're a ventro — a ventri —"

"A ventriloquist," Mr. Webster finished. And then, so we wouldn't be ashamed of having been fooled, he went on and told us stories about other people he'd fooled, making his voice come from all parts of the room. We had such fun that we didn't mind at all.

The next day, to show we were really still friends, we went back to see Mr. Webster. He was having lunch outdoors and Polly was squawking "Foaming action, foaming action," over and over again.

When Polly saw Clarence, she stopped the commercial and said, "Good dog, Clarence. Good dog, Clarence," which she'd picked up from Mr. Webster.

Clarence wagged his tail, but he was much more interested in Mr. Webster's lunch than in Polly. He took a seat beside Mr. Webster and looked hopefully at him.

"Would you like a cookie?" Mr. Webster asked Clarence.

Clarence pricked up his ears and wagged his tail, as good as saying, "Would I!"

Mr. Webster reached for the box.

Polly was still trying to catch Clarence's attention. "Nice pussy! Here, pussy, pussy, pussy!"

"Polly, stop that!" Mr. Webster snapped, opening the box.

"Here, pussy, pus — awk!" The cat had jumped to the table.

A burst of barking followed, and the cat fled.

"Ha-ha-ha!" Polly laughed.

"It won't be so funny when Clarence has gone back to Connecticut," Mr. Webster told Polly.

"But Clarence didn't bark," Brian said.

Mr. Webster looked down. Clarence was still sitting at his feet and staring at the cookie box.

We all looked at Polly.

Polly preened her feathers. "Nice pussy," she said — and barked.

There were no two ways about it. Clarence had taught Polly to bark. Instead of our having a talking dog, Mr. Webster had a barking bird.

6

Dogfish Or Fishing Dog?

Uncle Matt was going fishing. He stopped by the house to tell Aunt Jo and promised her "a great big mess of fish" for supper.

At first Aunt Jo was very pleased because it would save her a trip in town. Then a little shadow of doubt crossed her face. *"You're sure?"* she asked. "I don't have anything for supper — perhaps I should go anyway."

"Nonsense!" Uncle Matt said. "When I promise you a mess of fish, Josephine, they're as good as in the frying pan. The only thing you have to worry about is what you're going to do with so many fish." He caught sight of Brian and me behind Aunt Jo in the kitchen. "You two want to come along?" he invited.

"Could we?" Brian said. "Come on, Sis. Come on, Clarence."

Clarence bounded out the door and jumped up on Uncle Matt.

Uncle Matt shook his head. "Sorry, Clarence. No dogs today." He explained to Brian and me that fishing was a very serious business and not for dogs.

So we had to shut Clarence in the house. Brian patted him and promised we'd be back soon. Clarence drooped and all the bounce went out of him. He hates being left behind.

There were five or six fishermen at the wharf when we arrived, but no fish.

"How're they running?" Uncle Matt asked.

"They aren't," one of the men said. "Been here two hours and haven't even had a bite."

"Let some real fishermen show you how to do it," Uncle Matt said. He picked out a spot for us and set down the bait pot. He gave a hand line to me, another to Brian, and set out three himself.

Ten minutes passed, then thirty, then forty-five. Nothing happened. I began to feel a little sleepy sitting there in the sun, but Brian was starting to squirm. Suddenly he poked me. "Oh-oh," he said. "Look."

I looked.

Clarence was prancing onto the wharf and looking terribly pleased with himself for having escaped and tracked us. He was so happy that he jumped all over us and almost knocked the bait pot into the water.

Uncle Matt looked at Clarence and sighed.

"Maybe he'll bring us luck," Brian suggested.

Clarence sat between Brian and me and looked expectantly into the water. Nothing was happening. Like Brian, Clarence began to think this was pretty dull. He wandered off. First he tried to make friends with some of the fishermen, but nobody seemed to be in a very friendly mood. He sampled some chopped-up pieces of fish one man had brought for bait; the man chased him away. Then Clarence found a ball of twine. Very quietly he began to unroll it. Brian tried to take it away from him. Clarence decided Brian was trying to play tug-of-war, which is one of Clarence's favorite games.

At this point Uncle Matt suggested that perhaps the three of us might like to go exploring or something.

We walked to the shore and looked around. Brian spotted a big rowboat tied to one of the pilings under the wharf. In its bow was a basket of the kind used to hold lobsters when they're taken out of traps.

"Could we sit in the boat, Sis?" Brian asked. "Do you think anybody would mind?"

I didn't see what harm it would do. Brian climbed in. I handed him Clarence and climbed in myself. Clarence wasn't sure he liked this. The wooden seats weren't comfortable and there was about an inch of water in the bottom of the boat. Finally, Brian put Clarence in the lobster basket, where it was dry and more comfortable.

The next thing I knew, Brian had untied the boat. "Hey!" I said. "What are you doing?"

"I thought we could go for a little ride," Brian explained. "We don't have any oars, but I can push us from piling to piling. See?" He shoved off from one piling and caught the next. In this way we moved out to the far end of the wharf. Several fishing lines hung in front of us. Overhead all was still.

Clarence looked at the line by his nose. Inquiringly, he reached out a paw and touched it. Immediately someone overhead moved. The line jerked. Clarence stood up in his basket. He grasped the line in his teeth and tugged. Someone at the other end tugged back. Clarence was delighted. He braced his front paws and pulled.

"I've got a huge one!" a voice cried. "It must go thirty pounds. I hope the line will hold."

Brian was doubled up with silent laughter.

Clarence let go.

"Lost him," a disappointed voice said.

Brian reached out and tugged on another line.

"He's over here now," a different voice cried.

Brian gave the fisherman quite a battle before he let go. Then he reached for a third line.

"Brian, stop!" I whispered.

Brian looked at me. "Why?"

"They'll be furious if they find out."

"How are they going to find out?" Brian asked. He tugged on the line. "It's really a kindness," he went on. "Clarence and I are making the afternoon very exciting for them. Now they can talk about the ones that got away." He tugged again.

It was certainly true that there was plenty of excitement on the wharf. And in the snatches of conversation I heard, the fish-that-got-away seemed to be growing bigger and bigger every minute. Even so, I thought Brian had better stop.

"That's enough," I whispered.

Brian nodded. "I'll just give Uncle Matt a turn. He's got to have something to tell Aunt Jo."

Brian pushed the boat over to where we'd been fishing. Uncle Matt's three lines were hanging still. Brian looked thoughtfully at them. "I think Uncle Matt should have the most exciting fish-that-got-away of all," he whispered. He reached out and seized all three lines.

74

Clarence wasn't going to be left out. As Brian began to pull on the lines, Clarence joined in.

A roar went up from Uncle Matt. "I've got the granddaddy of them all! He's taken all three hooks."

Now the battle began in earnest. Brian and Clarence tugged with all their might. At the other end Uncle Matt tugged with all his might. Brian and Clarence found it hard to hang on. Brian kept clambering about, trying to brace himself. Clarence was growling softly.

"I've got to let go!" Brian gasped. "He's too strong." Then he said, "Sis, help!"

Somehow in the struggle Brian and Clarence had managed to tangle the lines around the basket handle. Slowly but surely, the basket—with Clarence in it—was being lifted out of the boat. I grabbed for it, but the basket and Clarence swung away.

"I've got him!" Uncle Matt cried. "I'll show you fellows a thing or two about fishing." He grunted. "A big one all right. Must run forty pounds. No, no—I can manage. Here he comes."

Beside me Brian swallowed hard.

Above, somebody hooted with laughter. Then there was a roar of men's voices.

"You show 'em, Matt."

"What a catch!"

"A dogfish!"

"What about that!"

"Shows what a *real* fisherman can do!"

"Clarence, Clarence," Uncle Matt said.

I let my breath out.

"He's safe!" Brian said.

A moment later Uncle Matt's face appeared upside down. "I thought so!" he said. "Come out of there."

By the time Brian pushed us ashore and tied up the boat, Uncle Matt and Clarence were waiting for us. Uncle Matt looked as if he didn't know whether to laugh or be angry.

Brian dug his toe in the sand. "I'm sorry, Uncle Matt. I was just trying to make some excitement for you."

Uncle Matt looked at him. "As your friend Miss Grimes would say, Humph!"

"I didn't mean for you to catch Clarence," Brian said. "I just wanted you to have the best fish-that-got-away."

The corners of Uncle Matt's mouth twitched. "Well, I can't be angry, because I've got to ask you to do me a favor. I'm going to catch it from Josie if I go home empty-handed. Would you and Sis go in town and see if you can buy us some fish?" Uncle Matt handed Brian a five-dollar bill.

"Sure, we would," Brian said, eager to make amends. "Come on, Sis. Come on, Clarence."

One of the fishermen was leaving, and he gave us a ride to town. But when we arrived at the fish store, there was a big sign on the door. It said: *Closed. Gone fishing*.

The fisherman shrugged. "That's the way it is around here. You could buy a steak, but first why don't you see what's going on at the dock? Maybe somebody's brought in some fish you could buy."

That seemed like a good idea. With Clarence at our heels, we walked over to the dock, where a group of people were clustered. Mr. and Mrs. Tolliver were off to one side. Mrs. Tolliver was working on a sketch of the harbor.

"Hi!" Mr. Tolliver called and waved. "What are you doing in town?"

Brian and I explained what had happened. Mr. Tolliver laughed so hard he had tears in his eyes. Then he said, "Well, I'm afraid you won't find any fish here. That's a pleasure boat over there, and I don't expect their fish is for sale." He explained to us what was going on.

At the end of the pier was a sturdy post with a kind of pulley at the top and a rope running through it. This was used to haul fish up out of a boat so that they could be measured and weighed. That was what was going on now. And people had gathered round to watch.

While we'd been talking, though, a change had
come over the watchers. At first they'd been idling
around. Now they were gathered in a group and all
looking at something. Some of the men were cheering. "Atta boy! You can do it! Come on — just a little
more."

"Say," Mr. Tolliver said. "That sounds like a big
one. Let's go see."

He found an opening in the crowd and pushed Brian
and me ahead of him. Brian is quite good at worming
through crowds. I followed him. Very soon we saw
what was interesting the crowd.

It was Clarence.

At first I thought he was just having another tug of
war. Then I saw that the rope he was tugging led

through the pulley in the post. There was something very heavy at the other end of it. Clarence had his front paws braced and he was slowly backing up. He hit a wet spot on the dock and lost ground, sliding forward. Gamely he began backing again. And all the while people were cheering him on. This time Clarence succeeded. Very slowly a large fish began to appear over the end of the dock. When most of the fish was in view, a man stepped forward and pulled it onto the dock. The rope went slack. Clarence looked a little puzzled. He gave the rope a shake. Nothing happened. He dropped the rope and strolled forward to inspect the fish.

"Well done, little dog," a pleasant-looking man said. "You worked harder to catch that fish than I did."

Brian and I stepped forward to claim Clarence.

"What's his name?" the man asked.

"Clarence," I said.

The man looked from Clarence to the fish. "I think," he said, "that Clarence deserves that fish."

"Hurrah!" someone shouted.

The man explained that he and his wife were cruising and couldn't possibly use all the fish they caught. All they wanted to do was weigh and measure this one. Then, if we could use it, we were welcome to it.

The fish was weighed. It was slightly heavier than Clarence. Our new friend explained that the pulley enabled Clarence to land such a heavy fish. Then his wife asked if we would like her to photograph Clarence with his fish.

She had one of those cameras that develop their own pictures. So in just a few minutes we had photos of Clarence and the fish. In one he was standing with a front paw on the fish. Another showed the fish on the scale, with Clarence looking very small beside it.

Then the Tollivers put the fish in the trunk of their car and drove us all home.

Uncle Matt was sitting on the porch with Aunt Jo. "Any luck?" he called.

"Wait till you see!" Brian yelled. He carried the fish over to the house in his arms.

"Great day in the morning!" Uncle Matt said. "I didn't ask you to buy out the whole shop."

"We didn't, we didn't!" Brian said.

"It's Clarence's fish," I said. "He caught it."

"And we have pictures to prove it," Brian said.

When he'd heard the whole story, Uncle Matt looked approvingly at Clarence. "First time I've ever been out-fished by a dog," he said. "You're a real cham-peen, Clarence, and hereafter you can go fishing with me any time."

Clarence was too tired to appreciate the praise. In fact, he was sound asleep.

7

A Pair of Old Sea Dogs

THE morning was gray and heavy and full of things that went wrong.

At the start, Brian, Clarence, and I were in the kitchen helping Aunt Jo prepare the lunch she was going to serve her bridge club. Or, to be exact, I was helping. Brian and Clarence were sampling things. However, as Brian pointed out, this is a very important job. If it hadn't been for him and Clarence, we wouldn't have learned that I put sugar in the deviled eggs instead of salt.

Then we made the mistake of leaving Clarence alone in the kitchen. He climbed on a chair and went on sampling by himself. The tuna-fish filling for the sandwiches turned out to be so good that Clarence finished it.

Next Brian poured himself a glass of chocolate milk and managed to spill it on Aunt Jo's best white tablecloth. By this time it was clear that Aunt Jo's patience was beginning to wear thin, but she didn't say a word. She just washed out the stain and spread the tablecloth on the grass to dry, hoping that she'd still be able to use it.

Not long after that, we heard her telephoning Uncle Matt. Aunt Jo's end of the conversation seemed to consist mostly of saying *"Please."* Finally, she came out into the back yard and, with a big smile, said that Uncle Matt had invited us to spend the day with him.

"Matt has an appointment to see a Mr. Baker from Boston this morning," Aunt Jo said. "Something to do with getting a job running a launch next summer. But you can go with him. He'll be along any minute for you."

Aunt Jo went back into the house. Brian and I wandered around to the front to wait for Uncle Matt. That was when we discovered what had happened to the tablecloth. Somebody with four dirty paws had walked all over it and was now sound asleep on the cloth, his stomach bulging with tuna fish.

Brian and I were still wondering how to tell Aunt Jo when Uncle Matt arrived. "Why such long faces?" he asked. "Aren't you glad to be getting away from all those women bridge players?"

Brian pointed silently to the cloth.

I told Uncle Matt what kind of morning we'd had.

"Clarence didn't mean to do this," Brian said, "but I think for once Aunt Jo is going to be angry."

"Hmmm," Uncle Matt said. "You have a point. Josie doesn't often lose her temper, but when she does —" He thought a little. "I've got it!"

Before we knew what was happening, Uncle Matt had dirtied his boots in a flower bed and then walked all over the tablecloth, carefully covering the paw prints with his own marks.

He stepped back and studied the cloth. "There," he said. "I'll say *I* did it. Happens I'm doing Josie a little favor today. So she can't get mad at me. I'll just go in now and confess." He strode into the house with Clarence at his heels.

We waited anxiously, listening so hard that we didn't even notice the stranger until he spoke to us.

"Excuse me," a voice said. "Does Captain Gregory live here?"

"He doesn't live here," Brian said, "but he *is* here. He's inside with Aunt Jo."

"He'll be out in a minute," I said. "Would you like to wait?"

"Thank you," the stranger said.

Brian asked, "Are you Mr. Baker? Is it about the job?"

I poked him because it wasn't really any of our business.

"Yes," Mr. Baker said. He looked down. "*What* happened to that tablecloth?"

"Clarence did it," Brian said, "but —"

At that moment Uncle Matt and Clarence appeared in the doorway, backing slowly onto the porch.

"Now, Josie," Uncle Matt was saying, "there's no need to carry on that way. I don't make a habit of it. I just don't know what came over me when I saw that cloth lying there so white and clean, but I had the most awful urge —"

Aunt Jo said something we didn't catch.

"Well, I just got carried away," Uncle Matt roared.

The screen door slammed. Uncle Matt stood staring at it. Brian ran across the lawn to tell him Mr. Baker was here. Meanwhile Mr. Baker had opened his notebook to a page headed *Capt. M. Gregory.* He put a mark beside the name. Then he crossed out the *M* and began to write in something else. At this point I realized it wasn't polite of me to be looking in his notebook, and I turned away.

Uncle Matt was coming toward us. "Mr. Baker? Glad to see you."

Mr. Baker shook hands without much enthusiasm and stepped away from Clarence, who was jumping up on him trying to make friends. "I was out this way, Captain Gregory, and thought perhaps I could save you the trip into town."

"That was right sociable of you," Uncle Matt said. "But I want to see the launch—that's a kind of boat," he explained to Brian and me.

"I don't think—" Mr. Baker said. "I mean, it really won't be necessary —"

"Of course it's necessary," Uncle Matt boomed. "Got to see if this new-fangled boat is safe for taking out tourists before I give you an answer, don't I? Besides," he added, "Josie wants all of us out from underfoot. Come on. You take your car and I'll take mine."

Mr. Baker gave up. He invited Brian and me to ride with him. Clarence started to come with us, but then Uncle Matt whistled for him. "You come with me," he said. "Can't leave me all by myself. There's no telling how many tablecloths I may tromp on without somebody to watch me."

Uncle Matt drove off first. Mr. Baker followed. He seemed deep in thought.

After a few minutes of silence, Brian said to me, "My, Aunt Jo was angry. Clarence would certainly—"

"Does he — ah — often do things like that?" Mr. Baker asked.

"Not really," I said, "and he didn't mean to. He didn't know it was a tablecloth."

"He probably thought it was an outdoor bed," Brian added.

"I don't see how anyone could mistake a tablecloth for a bed," Mr. Baker said rather sharply.

"It looks like a sheet," I explained.

Mr. Baker obviously didn't think this very likely.

"Clarence is very intelligent," Brian said a little angrily, "and I guess if *you* were down on all fours you might think a tablecloth was a sheet."

Mr. Baker choked.

I was beginning to be angry myself. After all, Clarence was none of Mr. Baker's business. So I said, "Clarence is so intelligent he once caught a burglar by untying his shoelaces. And another time when nobody was catching any fish, he got one by hooking it out of a boat."

Mr. Baker swallowed hard. "He's quite harmless, I suppose."

"Oh, yes," Brian said, "he's very friendly. He loves everybody." Forgetting to be angry, Brian chuckled.

"Soon after he arrived he got rid of a friend of Aunt Jo's by bringing back a dead fish every time she threw it away."

Mr. Baker didn't seem to see the joke.

"I mean," Brian said, "he was just trying to please her because he liked her and wanted to be friends."

Mr. Baker shook his head, as if to clear it. Finally he asked, "Did you say this happened soon after he *arrived?* I thought he lived around here."

"Oh, no," I said. "This vacation is the first time Clarence has ever been to Cape Cod or seen the ocean."

Mr. Baker pressed his lips into a thin line. "So he isn't exactly familiar with the water around here."

I didn't know what he meant by that.

Brian answered, saying, "He isn't familiar with any waters. He hates getting wet."

"I had understood," Mr. Baker said, "that he was a real —uh — sea dog."

"That's just a joke," Brian said. "You see —"

Brian never had a chance to explain, for we had arrived at the dock. We found Uncle Matt and Clarence sitting in a long, low boat with lots of seats.

"Nice little craft," Uncle Matt said to Mr. Baker. "I think I might just take that job next summer."

Mr. Baker turned pale and licked his lips. "What I

was trying to tell you, uh, Captain, was that the job is filled."

Uncle Matt's face fell. "What!" he exclaimed. "But your boss in Boston as good as told me it was mine. Who'd you get?"

"I can't tell you yet," Mr. Baker said.

Uncle Matt looked suspiciously at him. "There's nobody knows these waters the way I do."

"I'm sure that's true," Mr. Baker said in the voice of somebody humoring a small child. "But motors, you know — you old-timers used to sailing ships —"

"See here, young feller, I'm not so old as all that," Uncle Matt snapped. "I'm not exactly creeping around with a cane."

Mr. Baker looked pleadingly at us, as if he wanted our help.

Uncle Matt caught the look. "What have you two been saying about me?"

"Nothing!" Brian cried. "We never mentioned you, Uncle Matt. We talked about Clarence all the way to town."

"Uncle *Matt*? Clarence?" Mr. Baker said, bewildered. "You're not *Clarence* Gregory?"

It was quite clear who was called Clarence. At the sound of his name, Clarence stood up, wagged his tail, and tried to climb out of the boat.

Uncle Matt caught on and began to roar with laughter. Wiping his eyes, he said, "By Jupiter, if you thought I was called Clarence —"

Clarence gave Uncle Matt a worried look.

Uncle Matt rubbed him behind the ears. "Not that I don't consider Clarence a very fine name," he said.

Mr. Baker's face was crimson. "What about the tablecloth?" he asked.

"I told you Clarence did it," Brian said.

At last I saw what had gone wrong. "Uncle Matt offered to take the blame," I told Mr. Baker, "because Clarence was already in trouble with Aunt Jo."

Mr. Baker pursed his lips disapprovingly.

"So how about the job?" Uncle Matt asked. "Still open?"

"I'm not sure we really need a man of your experience, Captain," Mr. Baker said stiffly. "Not with a simple, foolproof little boat like this."

"It's the man, not the boat, that counts," Uncle Matt said.

"I'm sure it is," Mr. Baker replied, "but this boat is so easy to run even the children could handle it."

"Could we?" Brian interrupted. "Could Sis and I run the boat?" He climbed in and I followed.

"Yes, indeed," Mr. Baker said, "you just pull the handle on the end of that cord, put her in gear, and off you go."

Brian took a seat in the stern by the outboard motor. Clarence joined him.

"Tell you what, Captain. We'll just take a little run, and you'll see how dull the job would be." Mr. Baker cast off from the dock and jumped into the launch.

"Not on your life," Uncle Matt said. "Five minutes more and that fog will be so thick you won't see from one side of the launch to the other."

Mr. Baker laughed. "Surely an old sea dog isn't afraid of a little fog."

"Put back—" Uncle Matt began.

Just then several things happened in quick succession. Clarence discovered the little handle on the end of the cord. He took it in his mouth, shook it gently, then braced himself and tugged. The motor coughed, sputtered, and caught. "We're off," Brian cried and pushed the gear lever. We roared away from the dock.

"Golly, it *is* easy," Brian said. "Even Clarence can run the boat." He put his hand on the tiller. We began to zig-zag across the harbor. We skimmed past an oyster boat, cut under the bow of a yacht, and narrowly missed ramming a small sailboat at anchor. Clarence decided he didn't like boating. He shrank back as we whizzed past the other boats and whimpered when spray was flung back over the bow.

Uncle Matt reached the stern of the boat, grabbed the tiller from Brian, and cut our speed. "Be quiet now, till I get my bearings," Uncle Matt said. He listened intently. It was then I noticed how thick the fog had become. We could see each other, but that was all. Uncle Matt changed our course.

"How do you know where we're going?" I asked.

"By what I hear," Uncle Matt explained, "the bell buoy, the foghorn, automobile horns on shore. Baker," he ordered, "get up in the bow. If we start to ram something, fend us off."

Mr. Baker obeyed.

"Of all the fool things to do," Uncle Matt growled.

"I'm sorry, Uncle Matt," Brian said, "and so is Clarence. But Mr. Baker said we could run the boat."

"That's what I mean," Uncle Matt said.

"I didn't mean they *were* to do it," Mr. Baker said.

"Doesn't matter what you meant," Uncle Matt answered. "Any kid would take that as an invitation to run the boat."

The outboard began to sputter. Then it died. Uncle Matt tried unsuccessfully to start it.

"Out of gas," he said. "You got a spare tin of gas aboard?" he called to Mr. Baker.

"No," Mr. Baker called back.

Uncle Matt muttered something about people who didn't check gas tanks. Then he called, "Guess you and I will have to row."

"I don't think there are any oars aboard," Mr. Baker

said. "We don't even have a foghorn." He came back and sat with us. "What will happen to us?" he asked.

Uncle Matt sighed. "Reckon the tide will carry us out to sea. But don't you worry," he said to us. "The Coast Guard will find us out there as soon as the fog lifts."

When Uncle Matt stopped speaking, the silence closed in. We were wrapped in wet, gray fog that muffled even the slap of water against the boat. Clarence was shivering in my lap. I put my arms around him, which was very comforting. I tried to think about cheerful things, but somehow I kept wondering how Mother would feel if she knew and what would happen if the Coast Guard didn't find us. Time dragged on. The boat shifted under us as currents caught at it.

Uncle Matt stirred. "Getting near the mouth of the harbor," he said. "Hear how much louder the foghorn is?"

Clarence had noticed some time ago. He'd been squirming in my lap and whining from time to time. Now the sound was more than he could bear. He threw back his head. "Aourrou, aourrou!"

"Oooo, oooo!" the deep voice of the foghorn replied.

"Aourrou!" Clarence howled.

"Stop that!" Mr. Baker cried. "Can't you make him stop? It's bad enough without that awful howling!"

"Oooo, oooo!" the foghorn called.

"Aourrou-ou — ou-ou!"

"Leave him alone!" Uncle Matt snapped. He leaned over the side of the boat, listening.

Soon the rest of us heard a throbbing. Some place near us was a power boat.

"Oooo, oooo!"

"Aourrou, aourrou!"

The sound of the engines grew closer. "Ahoy!" a faint voice shouted.

"Ahoy!" Uncle Matt roared.

From then on things were very noisy with Uncle Matt yelling, Clarence howling, and the foghorn moaning. But nobody minded at all.

The dark shadow of a boat loomed up beside us. Hands reached down to help us aboard. The launch was taken in tow. We were safe and on our way to shore aboard a Coast Guard boat.

The captain of the boat told us that a fisherman had seen us take off into the fog. When we didn't come back in a few minutes, he called the Coast Guard. "Of course," the captain said, "I knew you wouldn't come to harm with an old sea dog like Matt aboard, but even so I thought I'd take a stab at picking you up on the radar."

"Did you?" Brian asked, studying the green blips on the radar screen.

"No, we found you because of your foghorn." The captain turned to Uncle Matt. "What kind of horn is that? It's wonderful — carries right through the fog. I'd like to have one aboard myself."

Uncle Matt grinned. "It's a very special foghorn. In fact, I don't know of any others just like it. Give us a toot on your siren," he suggested.

The siren wailed.

"Aourrou, aourrou!" Clarence howled.

The captain looked surprised. Then he said, "Well, there's a *real* sea dog."

Back on the dock Mr. Baker, who hadn't said a word all the way in, stepped up to Uncle Matt. "Captain Gregory, I've been very foolish today, but I hope you'll believe me when I say it would be an honor to have you in charge of our launch. And I'd be proud to shake your hand."

Uncle Matt shook hands and clapped Mr. Baker on the shoulder.

Mr. Baker bent and felt around in the fog. "Clarence, I'd be proud to shake your paw, too."

"I'll call Josie and tell her we'll be along as soon as we can find our way," Uncle Matt said. "She must be worrying." When he came back he was chuckling. "All is forgiven," he reported. "She's so glad we're safe that we can track up the house, walk over every tablecloth she owns, and skid the rugs up the walls, if we like. But I told her just to get the food on and set places for us and Clarence because," he said, pulling Clarence's ears, "all of us old sea dogs have got to stick together."

8

Farewell Gift

WE wanted to give Aunt Jo a present before we went home. Mother, of course, would send Aunt Jo a hostess gift, and our names would be on the card. But we had grown so fond of Aunt Jo that we wanted to give her a very special present, just from us. The only problem was finding exactly the right thing.

Finally, it was Aunt Jo herself who gave us an idea.

As the end of our stay drew near, she kept telling us how much she'd enjoyed having "two children and a dog," how much she would miss us, and how lonely the house would seem without us. So the present, we realized, should be something live, something to keep Aunt Jo company after we'd gone.

Naturally, it didn't take us long to decide that a dog would be best.

Brian gave the matter some thought. "We can't afford a pedigreed dog," he said, "but that doesn't matter. Aunt Jo would probably like a Clarence-type of dog best. And," he went on, "it should be a dog Clarence likes so that there'll be no problem if we come back for a visit next year."

I agreed. Now all we had to do was find a Clarence-type of dog that Clarence liked and that didn't cost more than five dollars and twenty-seven cents, which was all the money we had.

We started by digging out old newspapers and reading the FOR SALE ads. But the only puppies listed were pedigreed and cost a good deal more than we had to spend. Brian had another idea. He had seen a place for homeless dogs outside Provincetown. If there were any puppies, they wouldn't cost more than a couple of dollars.

Brian borrowed a bike and went off to see whether there were any puppies that might do. "If there are," he said, "you and Clarence and I will all go over tomorrow and choose one."

The trip took most of the afternoon. When Brian came back, he was hot and tired and discouraged. "No puppies," he reported. "Not even any young dogs."

I began to think about the FOR SALE ads again. Maybe if we wired Mother and asked her to lend us some money . . . Then I decided that wouldn't work. Mother would telephone Aunt Jo to see if we were in trouble, and when Aunt Jo found out why we needed the money she would insist that we weren't to buy her a present.

Meanwhile, Brian had taken the problem up with Clarence. "The trouble is," he was saying, "that you are a very rare and valuable kind of dog." Clarence wagged his tail, agreeing with every word. "Where are we going to find a Clarence-type of dog, hmmm? Could you help us?"

The expression on Clarence's face said that he would certainly like to help with whatever it was. But not being quite sure what was wanted, Clarence trotted away and came back with Fish. Clarence thinks there is nothing like a good game of Fish to cheer people up.

In the morning, Uncle Matt came by to say he was driving into Provincetown. Aunt Jo decided to go with him, but we said we'd stay home. We wanted to go on thinking about what to do. However, as things turned out, we didn't have much time. A few minutes later Clarence came home from his morning run, bringing a friend—a huge, white dog with pale tan spots, a pink

100

nose, and pinkish eyes. Her coat was long, wiry, and matted, and she'd been rolling in an oil slick on the beach.

Clarence sat down in front of us, bright-eyed, panting, and tail a-wag. The friend took a seat beside him, looked at us, and yawned.

"Hello, dog," Brian said.

Clarence's friend simply looked at him.

Brian held out his hand for the friend to sniff. This time the strange dog responded. She opened her mouth, Brian's hand vanished into it. The dog shook her head playfully. Eventually, Brian managed to get his hand back and wiped it on his pants.

Clarence was now at the back door, looking expectantly at us.

Brian opened the door for him. Clarence went in. Clarence's friend thrust herself between Brian and the door and went in, too. Brian staggered backward. "That's a big dog," he said. "We'd better catch her." So we all went in.

Clarence was showing his friend the house. She gamboled after him like a small horse. Brian followed the friend, catching ashtrays and other ornaments that the friend's tail swept off small tables. The tour ended in the kitchen. At Clarence's suggestion, we served dog biscuits and milk. The friend ate sixteen small dog biscuits and a large bowl of milk. Finally we managed to get them out of the house. The friend lay down on the front porch. It was clear that she approved of the house and the refreshments and had decided to stay.

Clarence was not only pleased with this situation but also expected to be praised. Brian petted him halfheartedly.

I looked at Brian.

Brian said, "Well, Mother always encourages *us* to bring our friends home."

Brian went over and spoke to the friend. She didn't stir. But her tail wagged when Brian patted her. "I wonder if she's deaf," Brian said to me. "She's perfectly friendly, but she just doesn't seem to know I'm talking to her."

I went over.

"She must have been in the woods," Brian went on. "She's full of ticks."

"I wonder if she belongs to someone," I said. "She has no collar, but she looks pretty well fed. I think I'll call Sergeant Wood and see if anyone has reported a lost dog."

I went into the house and telephoned. But the sergeant said no one had reported a huge, dirty white dog as lost.

When I came out, Brian was studying Clarence's

friend. "Sis," he said, "do you think Clarence could possibly have understood when I was telling him about our problem yesterday?"

"I don't see how he could have."

"Well, it's very strange," Brian said. "He's acting just as if he'd solved our problem for us. He's terribly pleased with himself and his friend. I wonder . . ."

Brian circled Clarence's friend a few times. "Do you think Aunt Jo would like her?"

"Brian!" I said. "That's not at all the kind of dog we wanted."

Brian backed off and looked at the strange dog through half-closed eyes. "There's no telling what she'd look like if we took the ticks off her and washed her and combed her. She might even turn out to be a Russian wolfhound or something. Besides," he said, "she's the only dog we have so far."

I half closed my eyes. Looked at that way, the dog did seem to have possibilities. "She doesn't have very much charm," I said.

"She may be shy," Brian said. "Probably she has lots of charm when you get to know her well. Clarence thinks she's awfully nice," he added.

That was true. Clarence was very taken with his new friend. "I suppose," I said slowly, "that Clarence is a better judge of dogs than we are. Maybe he's seen something we've missed."

"I'll tell you what," Brian said. "Let's clean her up and then see what we think."

I couldn't see any harm in that.

Brian said, "If we decide on her, we could use the money for a collar and license."

Cleaning up Clarence's friend was going to be quite a job. We'd have to start by de-ticking her. Brian filled a coffee tin with kerosene, to kill the ticks. Then we sat down in the sun and went to work. Clarence watched approvingly.

Luckily, the ticks were newly acquired and easy to take off. But even with two of us working at it, the job went on and on. Clarence's friend was very large and her coat was very thick. There is really a great deal to be said for a small dog with smooth hair, like Clarence.

We were still de-ticking when Uncle Matt's car drove up. Clarence proudly led Aunt Jo and Uncle Matt over to us. His friend was lying on her back while we worked on her stomach. She wagged her tail sociably and rolled her eyes at Aunt Jo.

"Jehoshaphat!" Uncle Matt said. "What's that?"

Brian scrambled to his feet. "This is Clarence's friend that he brought home." Brian looked down at us. "Of course," he said, "she's not at her best in that position. Up!" he said to the dog.

Brian rolled her onto her side. "I'm not sure she speaks English," he said.

Clarence's friend rose, shook herself, and stretched. Clarence stood up on his hind legs and touched his nose to hers. His friend's tail wagged.

"She has quite a lot of charm when you get to know her," Brian said. "Clarence thinks she's one of the nicest dogs he's ever met."

"I'm sure she is," Aunt Jo said kindly.

"I knew you'd like her," Brian said.

"What are you planning to do with her?" Uncle Matt asked.

"When we've finished de-ticking her, we're going to wash her and comb her," I said.

A look of suspicion crossed Uncle Matt's face. "You're going to all that trouble just because she's a friend of Clarence's?"

Before I could stop him, Brian had blurted out the truth. "When we get her all fixed up, we're going to give her to Aunt Jo so she won't be lonely when we've gone." Suddenly realizing what he'd done, Brian clapped a hand over his mouth. "It was going to be a surprise," his muffled voice said.

Aunt Jo and Uncle Matt looked at each other. Then Aunt Jo said, "That's a lovely idea, Brian! But surely such a fine dog must belong to someone."

"I called Sergeant Wood," I explained, "and he said no one had reported a lost dog like this."

106

We all stood in silence, looking at Clarence and his friend. Clarence took this as a compliment and wiggled with pleasure.

"Well," Aunt Jo said finally, "perhaps when she's washed and —"

"Josephine!" Uncle Matt said.

"Hush, Matt," Aunt Jo said, petting both Clarence and his friend.

Behind us car doors slammed. Sergeant Wood's voice said, "Now don't get your hopes up. I told you the description wasn't at all like —"

"Mopsy!" a short plump woman cried, running toward us.

Clarence's friend bounded toward the woman.

"Was' oo losted?" the woman said, hugging Mopsy.

"Huh!" Sergeant Wood said to us. "She comes into the police station saying she's lost her itty bitty doggy. No wonder I didn't think it was the same one Sis reported."

"And 'oose coatsie is full of nasty oil, poor 'ittle dog," Mopsy's owner said.

Brian made a terrible face. "Now we know why Clarence's friend didn't understand us," he said to me. "We don't speak the same language."

From Brian's point of view the worst was yet to come, for Mopsy's owner kissed Brian and Clarence and me while thanking us for having saved her itsy bitsy doggsy. Then, as we saw her into the car and said good-by to Mopsy, she gave us five dollars. We didn't want to take it, but she insisted.

Clarence didn't mind a bit that Mopsy had gone. His tail was up as he watched the car disappear. He was the perfect host seeing a guest off. He had, I guessed, just liked Mopsy and brought her home for a visit.

We went into the house with Uncle Matt and Aunt Jo. Uncle Matt drew the story out of us — how we'd wanted a very special present, how we'd decided on a dog, and the trouble we'd had finding one.

At the end, Aunt Jo hugged us and said it was the nicest idea any guest had ever had. But, she said, no matter how well Mopsy had turned out, it still wouldn't really have made up for our going home.

Uncle Matt gave us a big wink and said, "Josie, if you're going to be that lonely, maybe you should take me. I don't have ticks and I don't have to be addressed in baby talk."

From the look on Aunt Jo's face, I thought maybe this time she was going to say yes, if Uncle Matt would be serious. So Brian and Clarence and I went for a walk.

Now we were right back where we'd started except that we had *ten* dollars and twenty-seven cents. Suddenly I had an idea. I wondered if we could buy a drawing of Clarence from Mrs. Tolliver. I wasn't sure that we had enough money, but at least we could ask.

Brian liked that idea very much, and we headed off to see the Tollivers. I explained what we had in mind.

"Oh, dear," Mrs. Tolliver said, "I sold every single one of them to a man in Boston."

"But," Mr. Tolliver said, "there's no reason why you couldn't do a new drawing. How about one called 'Two Children and a Dog'?"

"That's a wonderful idea!" Mrs. Tolliver exclaimed. And she set right to work.

When the drawing was finished, it was just like the earlier ones. With only a few black lines, Mrs. Tolliver had put Brian and Clarence and me on paper. Anybody would have known us.

At first Mrs. Tolliver didn't want to take our money because she said we were all friends. But we explained that if she didn't, it would be her present, not ours. Mr. Tolliver sided with us, and so we ended up buying the drawing.

Aunt Jo thought it was perfect. This way, she said, it would be almost as if we hadn't gone away and she would have "two children and a dog" forever—as well as Uncle Matt.

The wedding was held at Thanksgiving so that we could all come. Clarence, of course, wasn't allowed to go to the actual ceremony. But he didn't mind because he was invited to the reception, and that's where the refreshments were.

Sea Dog at Home

CLARENCE was practically overcome with excitement at being home again. First he ran around the house three times, barking and barking. Then he ran through the house, investigating every room to make sure things were just as he remembered them. Finally he jumped into Mother's lap, partly to rest but mostly to show how happy he was to see her.

After he'd spent twenty minutes with Mother and refreshed himself with a drink of water, Clarence decided to explore the neighborhood and see if anything had changed while he was away. With a look that said he'd be right back, he banged open a screen door and ran off.

A few minutes later, the phone rang. Brian stopped in the middle of telling Mother about the time we were lost in the fog.

"Yes, they are," Mother said into the phone. ". . . just a few minutes ago. How did you know? . . . Oh, he did?" She covered the mouthpiece and said to us, "Clarence just paid the Brundages a flying visit." She turned back to the phone. "A hundred and twenty fish? Oh, you poor things! . . . I wish we could help, but we already have more fish than . . . Yes, they did . . . Yes . . . Well, thank you anyway, and I hope we'll see you soon."

"Golly," Brian said, when Mother had hung up, "did Mr. Brundage catch a hundred and twenty fish?"

"Yes," Mother said, "and brought them all home thinking the neighbors would like them. But Mr. Redstone and Mr. Wilson were also off on fishing trips and *they* came home yesterday. So the rest of us are already well supplied with fish."

"Did we write you about the time Clarence went fishing?" I asked.

Brian pulled out the photos of Clarence and his fish.

"Yes," Mother said, "but I'd love to hear the story again."

By the time Clarence returned, Mother was starting the dinner. Brian and I were upstairs unpacking.

Clarence dashed upstairs and began to help us, snatching something out of a suitcase, shaking it vigorously, throwing it down, and going back for something else. Then his mood suddenly changed. Thoughtfully he sniffed Brian's shell collection. Next he selected a salty, sandy sweater and sniffed it all over. When he'd finished, he lay down on it with a sigh and looked sadly at us.

Clarence was missing Cape Cod.

We told Mother about it at dinner. She said that this was nothing to worry about. Clarence would soon settle down to life in Fairport. "After all," she said, "he's spent his whole life here and only a month at Cape Cod."

Brian was still worried. "Maybe he likes being a sea dog," he said. "Maybe Clarence would rather be a sea dog than just an ordinary dog."

"It will be all right," Mother promised. "You'll see." Then, although she doesn't approve of feeding dogs at the table, she gave Clarence two bites of fish, without any bones, of course. Clarence immediately looked happier. Mother looked pleased that she had managed to cheer Clarence up.

But it was not as simple as that. Each day was full of disappointments for Clarence. Sandwiches in the morning didn't mean a picnic; they meant Brian and I were heading off to school. Clarence spent his evenings looking from us to the fireplace and back again; but Mother said firmly there would be no fires until winter. Worst of all, there was no one to take Clarence fishing or for runs on the beach or out in a boat. It was no wonder that the distant sound of a foghorn on Long Island Sound set him to howling.

After three hours of Clarence's howling, Mother was ready to admit defeat. "I don't know what we're going to do," she said, "but this can't go on. Clarence must pick up his old interests or develop a hobby or *something*."

As it happened, Clarence did develop a hobby the very next day. He took up gardening. However, it was a little time before we found this out. All we knew was that Clarence had found something to do that kept him busy and happy.

Very shortly, though, Mother had a new problem. She took me aside and said, "Sis, do you know if Brian brought home anything except his shell collection?"

"No," I said, trying to remember, "I don't think so."

"He didn't have a collection of — ah — fish?"

I shook my head. "Why?"

"Every now and then there's the most terrible smell of fish around here," Mother explained. "And this morning I found several fish heads on the lawn."

Now that she mentioned it, I remembered that I'd had several whiffs of fish myself. Just to be sure, I asked Brian if he'd brought home a collection of fish.

Brian denied it indignantly. "It's more like the kind of thing Clarence would do," he pointed out.

"Except," I said, "that Clarence couldn't have brought any fish home without our help."

Brian was staring thoughtfully out a window. "Look!" he said suddenly and pointed.

Clarence was trotting across the lawn, carrying something in his mouth. As we watched, he buried it in a flower bed and carefully filled in the hole. Then he lay down near the spot and sniffed the air. His tail wagged happily. After a few minutes, Clarence got up and ambled off.

Brian and I went out into the garden. It smelled faintly of fish. Brian dug where Clarence had dug. A few inches down he uncovered a medium-sized fish in an advanced state of decay.

"Ugh!" Brian exclaimed and hastily began to cover it with dirt again.

"Oh, Brian," Mother's voice said behind us. "That's not nice. It's not nice at all to keep dead fish in the garden."

"I'm not either!" Brian cried. "Why does everyone keep accusing me? It isn't at all the kind of thing I'd do."

116

Actually, it was quite easy to imagine Brian burying fish in the garden. But I said to Mother, "Clarence buried the fish." I looked around, noting other spots that looked dug in. "I think he's buried quite a few. Then he lies down and enjoys the smell. It probably reminds him of Cape Cod."

"That's very nice for Clarence," Mother said, "but not so nice for us. I'm afraid you'll have to stop him."

"But he's just doing what you said," Brian protested.

"What *I* said?" Mother exclaimed.

"Yes," Brian said. "You said he ought to develop a hobby. Now he's taken up gardening as a hobby—and you want him to stop."

Mother said weakly, "I'm not sure I want Clarence to take up gardening."

"You always say gardening is a fine, healthful hobby," I pointed out.

"And everyone should have a hobby," Brian said. "Hobbies are good for you and often very useful. Miss Gridley says so." Miss Gridley was Brian's homeroom teacher.

"Well," Mother said finally, "I suppose Clarence can have a hobby. But he's not to bury any more fish in the garden."

Brian shook his head. "You don't understand. Burying fish *is* the hobby."

"And," I said, "it's very good for the garden. The Indians always planted fish with their corn. We learned that in American history."

Mother gave in.

The only mystery left now was the source of Clarence's fish. It was solved that very evening when the Brundages telephoned. Mr. Brundage had had to bury his fish in a vacant lot near their house. Today Mrs. Brundage had seen Clarence digging up fish and carrying them away. She was worried in case he was eating them. Mother told her what Clarence was doing and then hung up, shaking her head. "A hundred and twenty fish," she said. "Oh, dear!"

Well, Clarence was happy with his hobby. And Brian and I were happy that Clarence was happy. That left Mother. She was happy that we were happy, but she just couldn't seem to work up any enthusiasm about Clarence's hobby.

Then Brian and I came home from school one day and caught sight of a strange car with Massachusetts plates parked in our driveway. Sure that some of our Cape Cod friends had come to call, we rushed into the house and followed the voices onto the porch.

Miss Grimes was sitting in the best chair talking with Mother.

"There they are!" she cried. "Children, aren't you glad to see me? Isn't this a surprise?" Fortunately, she didn't give us time to answer, but rushed on, "I just happened to be passing on my way to New York and thought it would be such fun to stop and see my seaside chums."

It was difficult to think of anything to say. Mother prompted us with a look. We went forward and shook hands.

"And where is dear little Clarence?" Miss Grimes inquired. "I thought he'd be with you. I've just been telling your mother about the grand times we all had together."

Brian winced.

"But I can stay only a few minutes and I did so want to see everyone."

"Brian, will you call Clarence?" Mother asked.

Brian went out onto the lawn and whistled. In a moment Clarence came running out of the bushes, and Brian brought him over to the porch.

Clarence was simply delighted to see his friend Miss Grimes. He jumped in her lap, licked her face, and tried to bite her nose.

"Clarence is certainly pleased to see you," Mother said.

"Animals and children just adore me," Miss Grimes said.

Brian was seized by a fit of coughing.

"I'm sure adults do, too," Mother said hastily.

"Ah-ha," Miss Grimes said, "well, I suppose some of them do."

Brian's coughing grew worse. Mother sent him in the house for a drink of water.

Clarence jumped off Miss Grimes's lap and dashed away at top speed.

Miss Grimes looked at her watch. "Now I've had this all-too-short visit, I must be on my way."

"It was very nice to meet you," Mother said. "The children have often spoken of you. I hope you'll stop again some time."

Miss Grimes consulted her watch again. "I wish I could stay longer now. But as it is, I shall be caught in the rush-hour traffic and probably be hours and hours getting to New York."

My eyes jumped to Mother's face. As I feared, she had caught the hint.

Miss Grimes said, "And I mustn't delay you from starting your dinner." Somehow the word "dinner" was the loudest one in the sentence.

My heart sank. I was sure that if she stayed to dinner, she would spend the night. And if she spent the night . . .

Mother opened her mouth to invite Miss Grimes to dinner.

I closed my eyes.

There was a patter of feet.

120

I opened my eyes and saw that Clarence was back. He had laid a large, ripe fish at Miss Grimes's feet and backed off. Tail wagging a mile a minute, he looked at Miss Grimes.

Miss Grimes turned pale.

"Clarence!" Mother said.

"Good dog, Clarence," Miss Grimes said weakly. "He has a splendid memory," she explained to Mother.

Mother invited Miss Grimes to dinner.

Miss Grimes hesitated, looking at Clarence and the fish.

"The children will take it away," Mother said pleasantly. "Brian!"

Brian came onto the porch and looked down. "Oh," he said, "Clarence remembered! He's got lots of other fish to show you, Miss Grimes. He has a hundred and twenty of them in the lot back of Brundages'."

Miss Grimes turned paler yet and came quickly to a decision. "You're very kind to urge me to stay this way, all of you," she said. "But I really must be on my

way or my friends in New York will start to worry."
Quickly shaking hands, she strode off to her car.

Clarence trotted at her heels, carrying the fish and
hoping to the very end that they were going to have
another fine game together. He didn't lose hope until
Miss Grimes's car had vanished from sight.

Somewhat to our surprise, Mother let Clarence
bury the fish in a rose bed and praised him for being a
good dog. "I know all about it," she said to us. "Aunt Jo
wrote me. Now I must write her and tell her about
Clarence's useful new hobby."

As things turned out, though, Clarence's new
hobby didn't last much longer. I guess you might say
Mother's good intentions put an end to it. She bought
a special treat for us old sea dogs. When Clarence saw
the treat he hastily withdrew from the kitchen into the
living room. The treat was lobsters, and they were
waving their claws.

Apparently Clarence did a little thinking after that.
He suddenly remembered that he was not only an old
sea dog but also a tracking dog, a watchdog, a
television-loving dog, and quite a few other kinds of
dog. Life went back to normal.

However, in the spring even Mother had to admit
that the garden came up better than ever, though for
some reason she did not encourage Clarence to take
up gardening again.